HER DARK SECRET

A BILLIONAIRE & A VIRGIN ROMANCE

MICHELLE LOVE

HOT AND STEAMY ROMANCE

CONTENTS

1. Chapter One   1
2. Chapter Two   5
3. Chapter Three   11
4. Chapter Four   25
5. Chapter Five   30
6. Chapter Six   40
7. Chapter Seven   46
8. Chapter Eight   52
9. Chapter Nine   57
10. Chapter Ten   67
11. Chapter Eleven   72
12. Chapter Twelve   77
13. Chapter Thirteen   83
14. Chapter Fourteen   88
15. Chapter Fifteen   94
16. Chapter Sixteen   98
17. Chapter Seventeen   104
18. Chapter Eighteen   110
19. Chapter Nineteen   118
20. Chapter Twenty   122
21. Chapter Twenty-One   127
22. Chapter Twenty-Two   135
23. Chapter Twenty-Three   139

About the Author   143

Made in "The United States" by:

Michelle Love

© Copyright 2021

ISBN: 978-1-64808-777-6

❀ Created with Vellum

1

CHAPTER ONE

Attico Fibonacci gazed out of the window of the jet as it crossed from France into Switzerland. Geneva lay below him, the Alps looming large as the jet circled and came down to land. He felt a slight tightness in his chest as he considered where he was going—his alma mater, the school he had left nearly twenty years ago, *L'Académie Amérique du Genève*.

As the plane landed, he pushed the thought of returning away and concentrated on why he was here—to give the commencement speech.

At almost forty, Attico Fibonacci could easily be called the most successful alumnus of the school, with the possible exception of his older brother, Tony. Both brothers had graduated with highest honors, fifteen years apart, and were the pride of their school. Tony, traveling to Geneva with his younger brother, had only good memories of the school. Attico, less so. Yes, he had been the 'it' boy, but then if his fellow students had known what had happened there ...

"Stop thinking about it," Tony said now, interrupting Attico's reverie. "It wasn't your fault, Atti, and it was over twenty years ago. Stop dwelling."

Attico nodded but said nothing. Easier said than done when you knew you'd ruined somebody's life. As if on cue, his cell phone buzzed. Lucinda, his now *ex*-girlfriend. "Hey, Lu."

"Hey, Atti." Thank God their split had been amicable—at least on the surface. "I just wanted to let you know that my lawyer has sent over the papers for the settlement."

"Good. I'll get them signed and back to you as soon as I get back to New York." He hesitated. "How are you?"

"I'm good," Lucinda said lightly and then there was an awkward pause. It might be amicable but it was still painful. "Bucky's missing you."

Their dog was an oversized German Shepherd, Bucky, of whom they shared custody. "Just Bucky?" Attico said softly and heard Lucinda sigh.

"Don't, Atti. Don't make this harder."

"I'm sorry. I miss you."

"I miss you too, baby, I do, but we both know this was for the best." Lucinda's voice was kind but firm. "You will always, *always* be my best friend."

"Right back at you, Lulu."

She chuckled but there was sadness in her voice. "I'll see you soon, Atti."

"Bye."

God, it still hurt. Lucinda had broken up with him almost a year ago after a six-year relationship. Attico had known, in his heart, that she was unhappy, that their relationship had turned to platonic friendship years before, but he had stuck his head in the sand until it became painfully clear that it was over.

He hadn't been able to see how he could ever love someone else after Lucinda. Grateful for the opportunity to leave New York for a few days, now as he got into the town car which would take them back to the Academy, he wondered if running away had been the best idea.

Beside him in the car, Tony gave a sigh. "Dude, I hope you perk up during this trip. You've been on a downer for months now. Attico, you're rich, single, and handsome. Live a little."

And he was right. Attico Fibonacci often appeared at the top of the "Most Eligible Bachelor" lists in the high-society magazines. A self-made billionaire in the property world, he was a gloriously good-looking man, tall, broad, bright green eyes, and dark, wild curls. Tony, older by fifteen years, was a dapper man with a shaved head, dark brown eyes, and an air of elegance whereas Attico was considered beautiful by both his peers and the women who flocked to him, his face both boyish and mesmerizing. He wore a light beard to make his face look his age, but even he knew the effect his looks had on both men and women. He wore a suit well, but he was more at home in blue jeans and a vintage tee.

Looking at the Fibonacci boys, no one would never guess they were brothers. Attico looked exactly like his father, Sebastiano, an Oliver Reed-lookalike with an air of wild menace and beauty. Tony took after their late mother, the serene and delicate Giovanna. But the brothers, despite their age difference, were devoted to each other. Tony was a confirmed bachelor, a lover of both men and women, who played the field, even now when he was in his mid-fifties. He could get away with it, his natural charm and extrovert tendencies making every transgression forgiven.

Attico, on the other hand, was surprisingly shy. He was a home-boy, preferring to spend time reading or walking the dog or watching television with someone. He eschewed parties, and that was one of the reasons he was now regretting agreeing to speak at his alma mater's commencement. There would be a reception afterward, and he was already dreading it, making nonsensical small talk with people he didn't know. God.

He must have given a sigh because he heard Tony make an irritated noise. "Atti, stop being a downer. Look at this place; it's paradise. After the hoo-ha is over, we're going out on the town and you're going to get laid, comprendé?"

"Whatever." Attico was aware he sounded like a sulky teenager and gave an apologetic smile. He didn't want to bring Tony down. "Sure, bro. Let's do it."

"That's more like it."

Attico smiled at his brother then, as the car turned a corner, he saw it. L'Académie Amérique, standing on the shores of Lake Geneva, a vast Belle époque chateau, home to the richest of the rich, less than two hundred of the world's most privileged students.

The setting for Attico's worst nightmare.

CHAPTER TWO

Temple Dubois wiped her brother's mouth and smiled at him. "All clean and tidy, Luc."

He smiled at her, his brown eyes alert and twinkling, but Temple knew he only saw her smile, not who she really was to him. The accident had made it impossible for Luc, and for almost twenty years, she had been the "lady that smiled" to him.

Not his sister. Not his caregiver. But "the lady with the smile." Temple could live with that. The doctors and nurses had told her that, for Luc, for him to be able to describe anyone like that was a miracle. The accident had stripped him of almost everything else—his ability to walk, to reason, and had robbed him of almost all of his speech.

"He might not remember you're his sister, his blood," the kindly doctor had told her a long time ago, "but somewhere in there, he knows and acknowledges that you are special to him."

Temple smiled at her brother now. The one thing the accident hadn't taken was his beauty, his sweet soul. Though he was older than her by almost twelve years, Temple now felt like the older sibling, having looked after him since she was eight years old, almost entirely by herself, with support from the Academy.

Now, as she kissed Luc goodbye and set off back to the Academy, she let out a deep breath. She had a week to herself after commencement before the summer school began and she intended to do ... nothing. She relished the thought of being alone in her tiny apartment in Geneva, the home she had finally been able to afford after years of living at the Academy, paying her way by teaching, and now she couldn't wait to escape to her own little haven.

She had a stack of books, plenty of good food and great music, and she intended to hole up and ignore the phone and all other humans—except for her daily visit to Luc, of course.

When she got back to the school, she went to her office, unlocking it, and she hadn't been back for more than five minutes when there was a knock and one of her students stuck her head around the door.

Temple smiled at her. "Hey, Zella, come in. What can I do for you?"

Zella, a gorgeous teenager with long dark hair and a thousand-watt smile, sat down opposite her. "A favor, and I know it's a long shot, but do you have a spare spot in your class for the summer?"

Temple's eyebrows shot up. "You're not going home?"

Zella rolled her eyes. "Mum's decided she's going to marry The Swede and their honeymoon is apparently a six-month long affair, so ... She said I could stay home alone, but honestly, I'd rather be here. Olivia, Barry and Rosario are staying. So ... any chance?"

Temple smiled at her. "I'm sure I can squeeze you in, but you know it's going to be pretty intensive, right? The exhibition we're studying is only going to be at the school for a couple of weeks, so we have field trips planned almost every day and classes afterward. Long days ... can you cope?"

"Pah, of course. It's going to be cool, right? First time the museum has allowed these items out to loan?"

The museum she was talking about was a small but prestigious museum specializing in Wiccan and occult artifacts and Temple was leading a special course for history geeks, as she called them. She nodded now. "Right. But you know that some of the items we're being loaned actually belonged to the school first?"

Zella nodded. "I heard. You know which ones?"

Temple grinned. "Spoilers."

"Aww, Temple ..."

Temple never stood on formality. She was Temple or Tem to both her colleagues and her students. It was one of the reasons she was so popular. "Nope, sorry, kiddo. All will be revealed in a week's time. Now, look, you've cleared staying with Facilities, right?"

"They told me I needed to confirm a place on the course first."

Temple scribbled out a note and signed it. "Here you go." She smiled at her student. Zella was one of *those* kids—bright, curious, smart, and collaborative. And kind, which was more of an issue than Temple ever expected when she started teaching. "Take that to Facilities and if they have any questions, get them to call me."

"Thanks, Temple, I appreciate it."

"Looking forward to commencement?"

Zella rolled her eyes. "It sounds like fun but I know it's going to be three minutes of excitement, and two hours of boredom."

"Yup, pretty much. See you later."

TEMPLE CLOSED up her office about 6:00 p.m. and walked through the halls to the refectory. Most of the students were in there and she grabbed some hot food and sat down with a bunch of them, chatting easily, trying to fend off questions about the exhibition from the lucky few who had enrolled in her class. If she had been honest with Zella earlier, she would have told her that the class had been full for weeks ... but it was *Zella*, and for summer school, Temple didn't mind playing favorites.

Someone nudged her on the back, then sat down by her. Nicolai Lamont, the school's professor of languages, and her best friend, grinned at her. "Hey babe."

Temple laughed. As always, his attempts at American slang in his thick French accent made her giggle—he did it on purpose now. "Hey, y'all."

Nicolai was her very best friend at the school—and Temple had always had a little crush on him, even if that crush was futile. Nicolai was very happily married to Rainer, a German artist and male model. Nicolai himself could have easily been straight out of an Abercrombie and Fitch catalogue for the silver fox generation. He was gorgeous, and most of the students had a crush on him. He and Temple had clicked the day he had arrived seven years ago when she was still a student, and their friendship was the most important thing in Temple's life, apart from Luc. With no other blood relatives, Nicolai *was* her family.

"Listen," he said now, nodding across the room to the dean's table. "Check out the hottie. I hear he's our speaker tomorrow."

Temple looked over to where he was pointing, and for a second, she felt her heart skip a beat. The dean was talking to a man in his late thirties, she guessed, who had the saddest eyes but was also the most beautiful man she had ever seen. His bright green eyes stood out against his dark olive skin and his dark hair. "That's Attico Fibonacci?"

"The one. Didn't expect him to be quite as delicious. Wonder which team he bats for?"

"Ha," Temple grinned. "He's *way* too beautiful to be straight."

Nicolai laughed loudly, which caused several people, including Fibonacci to glance over to their table. Temple's breath caught in her throat as Fibonacci met her gaze ... and held it. Temple felt that glance throughout her body. He didn't look away and neither could she. Temple became aware that the people around her were starting to murmur ... they too could feel the connection crackling in the air between her and this man.

It was too much. She pushed away her chair, breaking the connection, and walked quickly from the room. Nicolai caught up with her, his expression full of concern. "Hey, hey, are you all right? *Ça va?*"

"*Oui, ça va*. I'm okay." She shivered a little. "Walk me to my car, would you?"

"Of course." Nicolai still looked worried, but he walked with her to the parking lot. It was raining, not unusual here, and Temple apologized to him.

Nicolai shook his head. "It's doesn't matter, but tell me, little one ... do you know Fibonacci? Is that why you're upset?"

Temple shook her head. "No, I never met the man ... I'm sorry, just something freaked me out."

"What?"

She gave a half laugh, half sob. "I don't know. Forgive me, Nic. My head's a mess."

He hugged her. "Go home, get some sleep. And don't let Fibonacci get in your head. He's just a rich guy who thinks he can have every woman he sees."

Temple smiled gratefully at him. "Night, Nic."

"Night, Tem."

SHE DROVE HOME and locked the door behind her. She made herself some tea and sat on the window sill. Despite what she told Nic, it didn't take her any time to figure out why Attico Fibonacci's scrutiny had made her so uncomfortable.

A year ago. A night, rainy, like this one. Leaving a bar in Geneva after a night out with her colleagues. A handsome guy who had been making eyes at her all night. She had turned him down, politely.

He had been waiting for her outside.

She'd only just managed to fight him off before someone heard her screams and came to help. The police had been sympathetic but told her they couldn't locate her attacker. Temple had gone home and tried to reason with herself. She hadn't been raped. There was that at least. The one thing she had control over was the one thing that remained intact.

Her virginity. At twenty-eight, she kept it a secret, knowing people would be shocked. She knew people considered her beautiful although she herself could not see it. When she looked in the mirror, she could only see dark brown hair, dark brown eyes, and café au lait skin inherited from her Creole mother and her African-American father. She looked like her mom, soft, rounded. Her mom had been a noted beauty, but she had taught Temple that looks did not matter. Losing her when Temple was five, in a car wreck which had killed her father and her older sister, had been the worst day of her life until Luc's accident. That was when she had known she was truly alone.

So, tonight, as that beautiful man gazed at her, Temple felt a shift in her soul—and her body. It was as if she knew him, her body *knew* him and craved his touch. She shook her head now, feeling stupid. For the love of God, what could you tell from a look? Of all things, Temple did not believe in love at first sight, or even lust at first sight.

But the way her nipples had hardened and her sex had flooded with damp arousal ... "Stop it. Stop it now."

She thought it through logically. Fibonacci was only here for a day to give the commencement speech. She wouldn't even speak to him, despite the fact she had to be at the speech. The dean would command his beloved alumni's attention, she had no doubt.

She sighed with relief. It was paranoia, she thought, that's all. But when she went to bed that night, she couldn't help thinking about his startling green eyes and his beautiful face and knew Attico Fibonacci would haunt her dreams long after he left Geneva.

CHAPTER THREE

T ony knocked on Attico's door just after 9:00 a.m. the next day. Attico, half-shaved, let him in and Tony rolled his eyes. "Late again."

"We have four hours, Tony. Come in, I'm just shaving."

"Obviously." Tony walked into Attico's hotel room and looked around. "Huh. So, the blonde left already?"

"What blonde?"

"The cute blonde who was hitting on you in the bar last night." Tony made a face. "Atti, please tell me you got laid last night?"

Attico didn't answer his brother. They had been out late in one of Geneva's popular nightclubs, but all Attico had wanted to do was drink and then sleep. He still had a hangover now and squinted bloodshot eyes at his brother. "How do you look so good? You had more alcohol than I did."

"I've built up a tolerance, as could you, should you ever decide to lighten up." Tony sighed, brushing down his spotless suit pants. "What about that pretty teacher you had your eye on at the Academy? Did you find out who she was?"

"I didn't ask." Attico said shortly, and returned to the bathroom to finish shaving. He decided against taking his entire beard off but neatened it up. He liked the way it made him look less boyish, like he was someone that should be taken seriously, even if he himself didn't feel like he should.

"Jesus, Atti. Anyone would think you're in your eighties, not your forties."

"*Almost* forty, and at least I'm not acting like a teenager, Tony."

He heard Tony snicker and rolled his eyes. Tony could never take anything seriously. "How about you? Were you entertained last night?"

"Yes, thanks. They were both sweethearts and very discreet. Left early."

Attico sighed and wiped his damp face on a towel. The truth was that, last night, at dinner with the dean of the Academy, he'd been floored by how his body reacted to the young woman sitting at the table across the room. It had been a shock to his system to find himself aroused by her—she was so totally the opposite of Lucinda in every way, to look at, at least. Whereas Lucinda had a willowy, model-sized body, tall, with light blonde hair cut short, and was immaculately made-up, the women—the girl? She barely looked older than the students—was dressed casually in jeans and a faded pink T-shirt, her long dark hair mussed up and loose about her shoulders.

Her face ... God, her face was *exquisite*, and it was all Attico could do not to turn to the dean and ask who she was. Instead, he asked about the woman's neighbor. "I'm sure I recognize him."

"Nicolai Lamont," Dean Corke told him. "Professor of languages. He used to teach at Columbia and I know you've been attached to that school too, with your work with the younger people ... perhaps your paths crossed then?"

"That must be it," Attico lied smoothly, and was disappointed that the dean didn't take the hint and tell him who the beautiful woman was. They heard Lamont laugh loudly and Attico looked over to her table—and met her gaze. He held it, reading the myriad emotions in her lovely eyes, then started slightly as she pushed back her chair suddenly and left the room.

Everything in his body told her to run after her, but without causing a scene, it was impossible. And he hadn't wanted to frighten her; she was obviously upset about something and he was a stranger. He saw Nicolai Lamont go after her and felt a pang of jealousy. *Stupid. You don't even know her; you've no right to get jealous.*

But he couldn't get her out of his head and after drinking himself into a stupor last night, he'd caught a cab back to his hotel and had fallen asleep in front of the TV.

His head pounded with pain, so he threw back a couple of aspirin before following Tony out of the door. The ceremony was due to start at noon but Dean Corke had asked them to come meet some of the top students in the classes, including the valedictorian.

As the town car made its way around Lake Geneva to the Academy, Attico pulled a wad of papers from his pocket.

"That your speech?"

"Yup." Attico let out a long breath. "It's hokey and cheesy and nothing they haven't heard a million times before. The world is your oyster and all that crap."

"That's what they expect. If you turned up and recited the lyrics to "Baby Got Back," they'd object, I'm sure."

Attico's lips twitched. "Don't tempt me."

Tony grinned. "I'll pay you a million dollars to slip a lyric in."

"You're on."

Tony laughed. "That's more like it."

"Like what?"

"You. Man, I don't want to pile on but the last couple of months, you've been on a downer, which is understandable, but Dad and I were worried."

Attico sighed. "You talked to Dad?"

"Atti ... we still worry every time you get down some."

Attico shook his head but said nothing. He felt guilty, still, even after all these years about his breakdown, that terrible, *terrible* time back in his late teens when depression had consumed him. Despite this, it irritated him when Tony made more of the situation than he needed to. "Tony, anyone would be down after a breakup. Don't make a big deal out of it."

Tony was quiet, then nudged him. "Hey, is Lu still single?"

Attico gaped at him, then realized Tony was kidding. "Douchebag."

"Pussy."

Attico chuckled, his mood lightening. When they got to the Academy, Dean Corke came to greet them personally. "I hope you enjoyed Geneva's nightlife, gentlemen."

Tony and Attico exchanged a look and grinned. "Certainly."

Dean Corke took them through the day's schedule. "A drinks reception at 11:00 a.m. with the valedictorian and some of the staff, then at noon the ceremony. We'll have robes for you to wear, Mr. Fibonacci," he said to Attico, who smiled as Tony snickered.

"Fine."

The dean led them through the ancient halls of the school. Really, it was a beautiful building, all stone and sculpture. "Hogwarts," Tony had said yesterday as they had arrived. "I forgot we went to Hogwarts."

Attico was reminded of that now and so he was still smiling as the dean led him into the staffroom, a large, dark-wood paneled room with priceless artwork and an elaborate chandelier. Money was not a problem for this school.

Some of the teachers were introduced to him and Tony chatted easily—well, he made it *look* easy, anyway—to them as the drinks circulated. They were introduced to the valedictorian, a young African-American woman named Zella who shook their hands seriously but had a twinkle in her eyes. "So, if you're both alumni, you know all the secrets of the school? All the gossip?"

Dean Corke chuckled and Attico smiled a little uncomfortably.

"Not much to tell," Tony said smoothly, and Attico was grateful for the save. Dean Corke shot him a glance and Attico knew he, too, was relieved that Tony had brushed the question aside.

Twenty minutes later and Attico snuck a look at his watch. He was just contemplating a bathroom break, just to escape the throng of people, when he saw her.

Her dark hair was swept up into a messy bun at the nape of her neck, her curvaceous body poured into a dark burgundy dress which clung to the outline of her full breasts. A simple gold chain was around her neck and there was the barest minimum of makeup on her sweet face. As Attico watched, she skirted the edge of the party and headed for the drinks table. Shooting a look at the dean and Tony, who were deep in conversation, Attico moved quietly to her side.

"Hello," he said softly, and saw her start a little before she turned to him. Up close, he saw her eyes were a deep chocolate brown, there was a faint flush of pink on her cheeks, and her mouth was full, beautifully shaped, and a delicate shade of pink.

"Hello." Her voice was breathy and low, but without the annoying vocal fry so many women of his acquaintance used nowadays. Her large eyes studied him and Attico felt as if she were assessing him. He held out his hand.

"Attico Fibonacci."

She looked at his hand for a moment before shaking it—and he was sure she felt the same jolt as he did when his skin touched hers. "Temple Dubois."

Temple ... it suited her. "I'm speaking at commencement," he prompted when it became clear he would have to lead the conversation. "Do you teach here?"

"Sorry, sorry," she said, shaking herself and giving a nervous laugh. "I teach some of the history classes, mostly concentrating on artifacts. A geek," she said, with a sudden smile and he chuckled.

"Geeks are the best."

"You're an alumnus, I hear."

Attico nodded. "I am. Actually, it's exactly twenty years since I graduated this year."

Temple Dubois nodded, but he saw a wariness creep into her eyes —did she know the history of what had happened here back then? "Did you know Luc Monfils?"

Oh fuck. Don't lie. "I did. Terrible, what happened to him."

She nodded and looked away. "I came to live here shortly after that."

Attico was confused by the seeming change of subject. "You must have been very young to come here."

Temple shook her head. "It doesn't matter. Listen, I see Dean Corke heading over here, no doubt to collect you for your speech. Good luck with it."

"Thank you. It was good to meet you, Mademoiselle Dubois."

Temple smiled at him and his stomach constricted with desire. "Temple, please, and the same to you. Mr. Fibonacci."

He would have told her to call him Attico, but she was gone too quickly, and he felt bereft. God, she was beautiful, and there was something so vulnerable about her that made him want to wrap his arms around her and protect her from the world. He wanted to know more, but then Dean Corke hurried him away to get robed up and Attico had to push all thoughts of Temple Dubois to one side.

TEMPLE HERSELF HAD HAD to escape from Attico Fibonacci's company because she couldn't cope with the sensations his presence was sending throughout her body. Her skin felt aflame, her heart beat too fast, and a throbbing pulse beat between her legs. What the hell? She had never felt like that in a man's presence before and it made her a little panicky. It couldn't be a good thing, surely?

The man was a stranger, and now she knew—he had known Luc. He had been here when Luc had his accident. When the girl had been murdered. Attico Fibonacci had known her brother. It seemed fate that they'd met now, but did it follow that it was a good thing?

She was saved from dwelling on that fact as the commencement ceremony began and her students trooped up onto the stage to receive their degrees and their congratulations. Zella gave a rousing speech to her fellow students and friends, making Temple proud, and then it was Fibonacci's turn to talk.

Temple took the opportunity to study him. There was no doubt, she thought, that Attico Fibonacci was a sensational looking man, Hollywood superstar-looks, and he had a presence about him, something undefinable.

She felt a nudge and looked up to see Nicolai grinning at her as he sat down next to her. "Still eyeing the Fabulous Fibonacci? I have to admit, he's a looker."

Temple felt her face burn and Nicolai noticed, his grin widening. "You like him."

"I don't know him."

"Is he tingling your biscuits?"

Temple shoved her elbow into his side. "Shh, I'm trying to listen."

SHE WATCHED Attico as he gave his speech, which, while not earth-shattering and Kennedy-like, was interesting enough that she saw her students nodding along. As he drew to the end, she saw a twinkle come into his eye, a little mischief in his expression. "As for your future, I cannot lie, there will be chances and opportunities, but with them will come big 'buts.' An opportunity will arise, but you may have to take a drop in salary to do it or move somewhere away from your family. There will always be big 'buts' in every decision you make, I can't deny."

Temple half grinned. She saw Fibonacci's brother smothering a chuckle behind his hand and got it. She started to laugh quietly, and as she did, Attico looked over at her and smiled. God, cute, sexy, and *funny*. Damn it, he really was the full package, wasn't he?

SHE WAS STILL SMILING when she made her way down to the students who, released from the formality of the occasion, were chatting excitedly about the party later on.

Zella hugged Temple. "You are coming, right?"

"I am, of course, I want to be there for you all. God, I'm so proud of you all," Temple said to the small group of students with her. Barry, the blond quarterback-like sweetheart, grinned at her.

"Now that you're no longer our official tutor, can we admit our crushes on you?"

Temple rolled her eyes, chuckling. "Absolutely not, and don't forget, this summer school won't be a cakewalk. You want it on your transcripts, I'll make you work for it."

"Zel says you won't give anything away about the exhibit."

"Good." The voice came from behind her and Temple's colleague and deputy-dean, Brett Forrester appeared. The students murmured a greeting respectfully, and Temple nodded at Brett.

He smiled at her. "Temple, might have I have a moment of your time?"

"Of course, Deputy-Dean Forrester."

She winked at her students and followed Forrester out of the room. He was one of the few people who had been here longer than Temple, a man in his late forties who had gone from valedictorian to tutor to deputy dean. The rest of the staff were wary of his unhidden ambition, and even Dean Corke spoke to him with deference.

Temple was wary of him for a different reason. Brett Forrester was an attractive man, and he knew it, and he'd made overtures to her in the past, but Temple had always politely turned him down. "We work together, Brett," she'd said evenly. "And one of my rules is not to get involved with colleagues."

Now, though, she felt her heart sink. Brett smiled at her. "As you know, Temple, this semester is my last here at the Academy, but I will still be involved in the summer school."

"I didn't know that." Damn it.

Brett nodded. "Oh yes. The curator of the museum is a good friend of mine, and he asked me if I could oversee the loan of the artefacts."

Temple felt the sting. "He doesn't trust me?"

Brett gave a short laugh, putting his hand against the wall, leaning toward her. Temple backed off against the stone. "Don't worry, sweet Temple, there're no issues there. I just told him how close we were and that I'd be sitting in on some of the classes. That's all."

Nope. No. Not going to happen. "Brett, this class is very important to me, and to my students. There cannot be any distractions."

Brett smiled and leaned closer. "I look forward to working closely with you."

Ugh, slime ball. She pushed away from him, irked and pissed, but he grabbed her hand. "Come on, Temple. We both know this has been in the cards between us for years."

"What's been in the cards, Brett? You refusing to take no for an answer?" Temple had had enough now and Brett's face flashed with anger.

"You superior little whore. You've always thought yourself better than me."

Temple opened her mouth to reply, but then, out of the shadows at the end of the dark hallway, Attico Fibonacci stepped into the light. His brooding eyes were fixed on Brett, and Temple gave an involuntary shiver. Attico looked dangerous, more dangerous than she'd ever seen any man look. Dangerous and devastatingly sexy.

"*Bonsoir,*" he said evenly. "Mademoiselle Dubois, *ça va?*" His eyes dared Brett to answer for her.

"I'm fine, thank you, Mr. Fibonacci." Temple let the gratitude she felt make itself clear in her tone. Attico walked towards them. Brett, not wanting to give ground, edged closer to Temple, but Attico offered his arm to Temple, still looking at Brett.

"Shall we? I have reservations at Il Lago."

Temple didn't hesitate and took his arm. "I'm looking forward to it, thank you. Good night, Brett."

She wanted to laugh at the expression on his face. Brett wasn't anywhere near the same league as Attico Fibonacci and he knew it. Temple walked with Attico out to the front of the school, then turned to him. "Thank you, Mr. Fibonacci. I appreciate the rescue."

Attico grinned at her. "I thought you might. Brett Forrester is a sleaze."

"He is, and you probably saved me from an arrest too. He was about to get punched in the face." She gave a half-shocked laugh at her own words. "Not that I'm a violent person."

"Forrester could drive a person to it. I doubt anyone would blame you." He smiled at her. "And the invitation to dinner stands. I *do* have reservations at Il Lago. I'd be delighted if you would join me, but absolutely no pressure or obligation."

Temple gazed up at him. Every cell in her body was screaming at her to accept and she nodded. "I would like that."

Attico, to her surprise, looked relieved. *Really?* A man like him was nervous of asking *her* out? Come on ... this had to be an act ... didn't it?

"I'm very happy to hear that. I was driven here so I need to call a cab ..."

"Well, if you don't mind being driven by a woman in an ancient Volkswagen, my car is in the parking lot." She smiled back at him as he laughed. He was fun, certainly, and Temple found herself excited about spending more time with him.

"Lead on." He offered her his arm again—such a gentleman—and they walked to the parking lot. He chuckled when he saw her car. The pale blue Volkswagen Beetle was held together with rust and duct tape but Temple loved it. She grinned when she saw his amusement.

"I like big bugs and I cannot lie," she said to him, her tongue firmly in her cheek, and he laughed.

"Touché."

They got in as Temple shoved a handful of books from the passenger seat into the back. "Sorry, it's always an absolute pit."

"No, I like it."

"Also, the heating doesn't work."

"Always helpful in the Alps," Attico laughed, and she grinned.

"Sorry." She started the car, wincing when it gave a groan.

Attico chuckled. "Sure it's going to make it into the city?"

"Oh ye of little faith." She turned to him. "Sure you don't have to tell anyone you're leaving? Your brother? The dean?"

Attico smiled. "I'm my own man. I've done what they asked of me. Now I get to enjoy myself."

Temple let the car idle while she studied him. "Mr. Fibonacci ..."

"Attico."

"Attico ... me agreeing to dinner is just that. *Dinner.* So, if you're expecting anything else ..."

He held up his hands. "I'm just grateful you agreed to dinner, Temple. I'm not expecting anything."

Temple felt relief—and not a little disappointment at his words. He was glorious, but if he thought she would leap straight into bed with him, he had another thing coming ...

however tempting that prospect might be.

TEMPLE DROVE INTO THE CITY, and he directed her to the hotel. Il Lago was at the Four Seasons Hotel and Temple's eyes widened as Attico led her inside. "I think I'm underdressed."

It was Attico's opinion that she was far too *over*dressed for his liking but he kept that to himself. He sensed Temple would not be comfortable if he told her honestly what her presence, her company, the scent of her skin was doing to his body. That her clean, fresh perfume was driving him crazy, that the heat of her hand on his arm made him want to pull her into the darkest alcove here and kiss her until they were both breathless.

Instead he pulled out her chair for her, smiled as she thanked him, and sat down opposite her. "Well, this is a very unexpected pleasure," he said and chuckled. "I promise you, I don't often do this."

Temple looked at him skeptically and he held up his hands. "It's true, despite what the papers might say. I was in a long-term relationship for years and since that ended, I've not been on a date."

"Who said this was a date?" But she was grinning, and he chuckled.

"Touché. *Again.*"

"Did you enjoy today?" Temple thanked him as he handed her a menu and nodded when he asked her if red wine was okay.

"I'm not a huge fan of public speaking, but it was ..." He thought for a second. "It was interesting to be back here again."

"You haven't returned since your own graduation." Temple colored a little. "I would have remembered."

Attico held her gaze. "Now I wish I had."

They stared at each other for a long moment, then Attico grinned and Temple laughed. "It's going to be one of those conversations, isn't it? Double meanings in everything we say ..."

"... and awkward flirting from me," Attico said ruefully.

"You, awkward? I can't see that." Temple smiled at him. "No one that looks like you could ever be awkward."

"I may just surprise you, Temple Dubois. Tell me ... how come you've lived at the school for so long?"

Temple hesitated, and he was sad to see wariness creep into her eyes. "My family ... I was alone, suddenly, when I was eight. The school—" She trailed off and shook her head as if arguing with herself. "The school bore some responsibility for that. I had been living here with my older brother—"

Suddenly Attico got it. With a sinking heart, he closed his eyes and nodded. "Luc."

"Yes. Luc is my brother. As you know, he was accused of murdering a young woman, amongst other things, and he tried to commit suicide."

Attico's heart was pounding. "I know. God, Temple, I'm so sorry. Luc was ..."

Temple gave a rueful smile. "Can't quite say 'innocent, can you? It's okay, the evidence was pretty damning."

A cloud had settled over their table and Attico risked touching the back of her hand lightly. "I am sorry, Temple, I really am."

"There's been a lot of rumors over the years but no one who seems to know what the hell was going on back then."

"What kind of rumors?" Attico felt dismay in his heart that this lovely young woman had had to live with this horror all these years.

"About a secret society Luc was involved in ... Look, sorry, it's not exactly cheerful dinner conversation, I'm sorry. Let's change the subject."

She smiled at him, but Attico knew then he could not pursue any sort of relationship with her. He knew too much ... he had *done* too much ... and this was his penance.

Goddamn it ...

TEMPLE NOTICED the change in Attico's mood and wondered if she had done the right thing by telling him so much. He had been there —maybe reminding him of what happened had been the wrong thing, but she had a hard time lying to someone who had been there, someone who could tell her what it was like ...

But she felt tearful now as the atmosphere between them changed. The dinner was excellent, and they chatted easily still, but the heat that had been there was gone. Attico offered to escort her home, but she politely declined. "Thank you for dinner, Attico."

He kissed her cheek, leaving her skin burning. "It was an honor to meet you, Temple."

And he was gone. Temple sighed and started her car, driving home, then clumping despondently up her stairs to her apartment.

"Dammit," she said, throwing her purse on the couch. She felt so deflated. "Why did you get so heavy? You scared him away!"

But the need to have her questions answered by someone who had been there when Luc ...

No. She pushed the thought away. Attico Fibonacci had been a pleasant diversion for an evening, but that was it. He was neither the answer to her questions, nor a potential lover. *First* lover. Temple groaned and buried her face in a pillow. She knew now what it felt like to be so turned on by someone that her body felt like it was crying out for his touch. She clutched the pillow tightly and let herself imagine what it would have been like to make love to Attico.

Those eyes, that heavy, brooding brow of his sending shivers up and down her body as he approached, those long, well-manicured fingers on her body, sliding her dress from her shoulders. His strong legs, the broad shoulders, that mouth, that sensual mouth on her own, then on her body, moving down ...

"Stop it!" she growled into the pillow, then threw it across the room. *Stop acting like a child.* Attico Fibonacci wasn't just out of her league, he was in a whole different solar system, and the fact that she had told him she wasn't going to sleep with him just because he bought her dinner ... well, he'd lost all interest, clearly.

Sighing, Temple got up and went to her bedroom, stripping off before going to take a shower. Later, in bed, she read for a while before falling asleep and dreaming of being naked with Attico and giving up all of her inhibitions as he made sweet love to her ...

CHAPTER FOUR

Attico thanked the driver as he stepped out of the town car into the airport. Tony was ahead of him, all ready to board their private jet, but Attico felt almost bereft. He hadn't looked forward to coming here in the first place but now it felt like he had unfinished business.

Temple Dubois. He couldn't get her out of his head, both because he was attracted to her physically, and also because he was someone who had known her brother, Luc, before his accident. He, Attico, could help her find the answers she was looking for ... but it would cost him. It would cost him a lot.

"Hey, douchebag, you ready?"

Sometimes it was easy to forget that Tony was a fifty-five-year-old man. Attico gave him the finger and smiled. "Just reminiscing."

"About the hot teacher? Yeah, I know you hooked up with her last night."

"We had dinner, and that's all."

Tony rolled his eyes. "It was on a silver platter and you didn't go for it?"

Attico felt irked at Tony's disrespect for Temple. "Mademoiselle Dubois is a class act, Tony. I'm not surprised you didn't recognize it."

"Oo, bitch." Tony was amused, but when he saw Attico wasn't smiling, he relented. "You like her, huh?"

Attico nodded. "But there's no future there."

Tony waited until they were on the jet before he spoke again. "Why, Atti? You've not looked at another woman since Lucinda, and now that you've met this teacher girl—"

"Her brother is Luc Monfils."

Understanding crossed Tony's face. "Ah."

"So, you can see why I'm not pursuing this."

Tony half smiled. "Even though you like her."

"She's beautiful, smart, funny ... and I helped destroy her life."

"Atti."

Attico shook his head. "Don't. Just don't."

Tony sighed but stay silent. Attico stared out of the window as the jet moved down the runaway, getting into position for lift off. Temple Dubois had been a sweet diversion but there was no way he could stay and see if their attraction led to anything.

No way.

THE WEEK TEMPLE spent reading and chilling out had been welcomed but now she was ready to teach her classes for the summer. It helped, too, that preparing her lessons had distracted her from the fact that she hadn't heard from Attico Fibonacci after that one night. She had to admit—it hurt a little, but, she reasoned, some people just drop into your life for a brief moment and change your outlook.

And he had. Just for the one night, he had made her feel interesting, beautiful, feminine. Desirable. *A gorgeous man wanted me*, she said to herself and smiled. Even if nothing had come of it, it was still a good feeling.

Now, as she made her way to her lecture theater, she was smiling and didn't see Brett Forrester appear beside her until he spoke. "Did you enjoy your date with Fibonacci?"

Temple sighed. "That's none of your business, Brett."

He smiled thinly. "You know, I might be leaving the school after the summer, but I still have some sway with the dean. You might want to be nicer to me."

"I don't respond to threats, Deputy-Dean," Temple said, her voice clear and loud so that the students could hear her, and Brett backed off with a supercilious smile. He sat down at the back of the class and Temple sighed. *Just ignore him.*

She smiled at her students. "Hey all, thanks for enrolling in this class. Obviously, it's outside the normal curriculum, but it will be a credit that you can show on your academic transcripts."

Temple perched on the edge of her desk. "So, as you all know, the Museum D'Nuit has loaned the school some of its more controversial artefacts for an exhibition here in a couple of weeks. The art faculty has very kindly allowed us access to the artifacts before they go on show, so you'll get up close, physical access."

She grinned at her students. "Now I know some of the more curious—or nosy—of you have already been guessing as to which items we're getting and yes, now I can confirm we will be getting a close look at *Le Tarot Du Sang D'Hiver*—the Tarot of Winter Blood."

A small rumble of appreciation went through the class and Temple chuckled. "Now, for those of you who don't know, the tarot deck is one of the oldest ever discovered, and it was discovered right here, at the Academy, during building work around twenty-two years ago."

She turned to her laptop and cued up an image of a tarot card. It depicted a woman blindfolded and tied to a stake with a demonic figure dancing around her. "This is one of the few cards which doesn't show actual violence. As you know, the deck is controversial for its depictions of graphic violence and is considered one of the most misogynistic decks ever produced. For that reason, the school gave it away to the museum, where it has been the subject of protests and controversy, for obvious reasons."

One of her students put his hand up. "Yes, Damon?"

Damon, a jock from New England money, smiled. "Will we get to see the whole deck? Even the Major Arcana?"

"Of course. The dean has given his permission and, as you are all over eighteen, we didn't need permission from your parents, although I certainly hope you discussed this with them. I know some people had concerns over the occult nature of some of these artifacts, but as we made clear, this isn't a class which deals with beliefs. This is purely art history."

Temple ran through some of the other items they'd be studying for the rest of the class and set up a schedule for them to visit the exhibition. "Obviously, usual rules apply, no cell phones, cameras, gum, or liquids near the pieces, please."

"The school expects you all to be on your best behavior," Brett Forrester spoke up from the back of the room, prompting eye rolls from most of the class.

"Well, as we're all adults here ..." Temple said, flint in her voice as she glared at him.

"Temple?" Rosario de Silva raised her hand and Temple smiled at her.

"Yes, hon?"

"Is it true that the deck was linked to a murder back in the day?"

Temple felt her chest tighten. She'd been expecting the question. "That's something we'll be discussing when we actually see the pieces. Okay, for now, class dismissed. Thanks everyone."

SHE MADE her way back to her office, avoiding an approaching Brett, and shutting the door behind her. Her eyes widened when she saw the flowers on her desk. Who ...?

Somehow, as she opened the card, she knew.

I CAN'T STOP THINKING *about you, Temple Dubois.*
 Attico Fibonacci.

IN THE ENVELOPE, too, was another small card—an invitation to an art exhibition in Paris at the weekend.

. . .

SAY YES AND I'll send the jet to pick you up. Say yes, Temple.

TEMPLE FELT her face burn and her stomach curl with pleasure and surprise. *Wow.* The thought of seeing him again made her body ache, yearn, even though in reality, he was still a stranger to her.

His cell phone number was on the card and before she could talk herself out of it, she called him. He answered on the first ring. "Hello, Temple."

"Yes," she said, almost breathless. "Yes, I will come to Paris."

"Good," Attico said, and again she sensed his relief. "I can't wait to see you again."

"Just so you know ..."

"I'm not expecting anything but your company, sweetheart, I swear." God, his deep voice made her belly squirm with desire.

"So we're clear."

He chuckled. "We are. I just wanted to see you again."

"Paris."

"I can't wait. See you at the weekend."

CHAPTER FIVE

ew York...

ATTICO ENDED the call with the biggest smile on his face. It had been a week since he had seen her and it was too long. He hadn't talked about it with Tony, but this morning, on impulse he'd had the idea. A friend of his, Maceo Bartoli, was holding an exhibition in Paris at his new gallery, and seeing the invitation on his desk, Attico had known he wanted to invite Temple.

Now she had agreed, and he called his assistant, Jeph, in to arrange the private jet. Jeph, a slinky hipster from Queens, grinned at him. "Gossip?"

Attico rolled his eyes. He and Jeph had worked together for so long now that they were almost family and Attico was always amused at Jeph's penchant for gossiping.

"Met a cute girl in Switzerland."

Jeph's eyes lit up. "Goody. Tell me more."

"Not much to tell yet, except she's agreed to fly to Paris to meet me this weekend. Can you send the jet?"

He gave Jeph all the details and his assistant got up to leave the room. "Oh wait." He turned back to Attico, and this time he wasn't smiling. "I saw Lucinda at George the other night."

Attico sighed. What now? Jeph seemed hesitant. "Atti ... she's pregnant."

Ouch. Like a brick bat to the chest. "Well ... I hope she's happy," he said evenly, nodding at Jeph. Jeph read the signal to leave Attico alone and closed the door quietly behind him.

Attico turned his chair to look out over Manhattan. *Pregnant.* How many years had they tried and not been successful and now, within months, she was pregnant?

"Fuck." He said it quietly, but the pain was real. He longed for a child—something he hadn't confided to anyone, *ever.* Every month he had been with Lucinda, he'd been so excited for her to say that she was late, that she had taken a test and that they were going to be parents. He was almost forty—he wanted kids soon so that he was still fit and able enough to play and run with them.

He glanced at the clock. He had a late meeting with some clients tonight, but until then ... he grabbed his bag and headed out. He drove to his gym and worked out, getting all the frustration he felt out. On the treadmill, he stuck his earbuds into his ears and turned the music up as he ran for miles.

After a half hour, he slowed his pace, noticing that there was only one other person using the facilities, a middle-aged man whom he'd only recently seen using the facilities. Attico nodded politely.

"Hey there." The man was puffing on the adjacent treadmill and Attico had the strange idea that he'd been trying to keep pace with him.

"Hey." Attico wiped his face and stepped off the treadmill. It wasn't usual for the gym's clientele to start conversations and so he was surprised when the man slowed his own pace and smiled at him.

"Denny Fleet." He stuck his hand out and, not wanting to be rude, Attico shook it.

"Attico Fibonacci."

"Oh, I know. You're famous around here. The new building on Fifth is spectacular."

Attico gave him a polite smile. "Thank you, but it's really down to the architects on my team."

"Ah, don't put yourself down. I've seen your other work, here, Seattle, Chicago. Big fan."

"You follow property?"

Denny nodded. "I do. Frustrated architect. Family wanted me to go into banking, always regretted it."

"Never too late to change."

"Ah, I don't know. Anyway, good to meet you."

"You too."

Attico finished his workout and headed for the showers. As he left the gym parking lot a while later, he didn't see the car following him, nor when it parked outside his offices. The driver watched him as Attico went inside, then silently pulled away and drove off into the night.

Geneva

TEMPLE FOLLOWED her students into the exhibition hall where artifacts they were to study were laid out. As she predicted, her entire class made a beeline for the tarot display. Temple steeled herself for what she expected to be a wave of distress. She knew the cards were graphic but even she wasn't prepared for how macabre they were. *Jesus,* she thought, *they're horrific.*

Each of the four suites of the deck—*Wands, Cups, Swords,* and *Pentacles*—had scenes of debauchery, deviancy, and violence but it was the twelve cards of the Major Arcana which were truly shocking. Each showed a murder, each one a helpless woman bound and tied, run through with daggers and swords. Even the positive cards

—*Justice, The Lovers*, for example, had their meaning twisted and sullied.

Temple gathered herself, aware she was gaping. Not a good look for the teacher. "Okay, so … obviously this is the Tarot of Winter Blood or *Le Tarot Du Sang D'Hiver*. Now, despite its French-sounding name, it actually follows the Italian-style of four suits with wands, cups, swords, and pentacles, and is believed to have been created in the late fifteenth century. By whom, we don't know, but I think we can safely say that this does count as an occult deck, rather than one for card games."

"Temple?" Zella, like the rest of the class, looked a little shaken. "Why would anyone … I mean, this is sick."

"It is, but then again we've talked before about historical perversion, too. Emperor Tiberius at *Villa Jovis*, the Babylonians, Caligula …"

"But this is so … why are all the victims women?" This was Rosario now, her voice shaking, as she studied the cards. Despite their age

"Why are they always?" Zella muttered and Temple nodded.

"'Twas ever thus, I agree, but we'll be researching into its history and hopefully unpacking some of the …" she looked down at the cards, "the *hatred* behind these things."

LATER, as she sat alone at home, planning her next week's lessons, her cellphone bleeped.

Hello.

She grinned. Attico. *And hello to you too.*

I didn't know whether I should text you, or if that would be an intrusion.

Temple laughed and called him back. "You're flying me to Paris. I think it's okay that you text me. Or call me."

Attico laughed. "You have a point. How are you?"

"Good, thank you. Teaching summer school. It's only a couple of classes a week but it keeps me in new pencils." God, she sounded like an old woman. "Or, you know, something cooler."

"Hey, no, I'm with you on the pencils—still love the smell of them when they're freshly shaved ... okay, that just sounds wrong."

Temple giggled. "Or you have a dirty mind."

"That too. But I do mean it about the pencils."

"You liked school?"

"Loved it, most of the time."

"Geek."

Attico chuckled. "You know it. I'm looking forward to seeing you again, Temple."

"Me too. Um ... there was something I wanted to ask you?"

"We've booked you a room, Temple, at the George V. A *separate* room. I told you, I'm asking for nothing but your company to the exhibit, I swear to you."

"Thank you." Temple wished he could see her smile. "You are a gentleman, Attico Fibonacci."

"I try. I know the crap men try to pull, especially some of my peers, who think money buys them whatever and whoever they want. If I have to keep proving to you I'm not one of those guys, I will."

Temple felt her chest warm at his words. "You're already halfway there," she said softly, and heard him laugh.

"I hope so."

Temple closed her eyes. "I can't wait to see you," she said, before she could stop herself, but then knew it was the truth.

"Me either," Attico said. "Two days, Temple."

"Two days."

THE NEXT DAY, she went to visit Luc at the hospital and was surprised to see him laughing and chatty. These were rare days when he seemed almost like his old self. "Temple, he came. He came today."

Temple frowned. "Who came, boo?"

"Him. He told me he was looking after you, that he always cares for you. He's nice."

Temple questioned him about his mysterious visitor but Luc just shook his head and called the man "him," getting irritated when Temple pressed him.

"Just him," he snapped at her and turned away, a thin stream of drool escaping from his lip. Temple wiped it for him and changed the subject but later, after Luc had fallen asleep, she went to see the nurses and asked them who had come to see her brother.

TWENTY MINUTES later she was driving back to the academy, ignoring the speed restrictions, her teeth set and her temper high. *Bastard. Utter, utter bastard.*

She stomped her way to Brett Forrester's office and didn't bother to knock. The sight of Forrester, pants down, fucking one of the teaching assistants stopped her in her tracks, however. The teaching assistant, Delia something, shrieked with fright but Temple was too riled up to care.

"Get out," she barked at the women, who grabbed her clothes and ran. Brett, not fazed at all, smirked as he tucked his fading erection back into his underwear and zipped his pants up.

"Really, Temple, if you wanted a threesome, you only had to ask."

"Shut your mouth, Forrester. Shut your goddamned mouth. How dare you intrude on my private life?"

"I'm sure I don't know what you mean." But still the smile remained and Temple wanted to punch it off his smug face.

"You don't go to see my brother. He's nothing to do with this school, nothing to do with you. How dare you?"

He moved so quickly she didn't have time to move and, in a flash, Brett had Temple pinned against his wall. "You ungrateful little bitch. You have no idea what I've done for you, for your brother. It's about time you showed me some gratitude."

His hands were under her skirt, moving up her thighs. Temple stamped on his instep and he let her go, roaring in pain. Temple tried to duck the fist that came her way but it connected with her jaw and she was thrown across Brett's desk. He grabbed her and pushed her down on her stomach, kicking her legs apart. "Gratitude," he growled as he yanked up her skirt and pulled her panties down.

Temple screamed, struggling as Brett pushed her down, then suddenly she felt him released her as another voice roared with anger. She struggled around, pulling her skirt over her buttocks to see Attico Fibonacci throwing Brett across the room. Brett was no match for Attico's size and he crumpled as he slammed into the stone wall.

Attico was next to Temple in a flash, lifting her into his arms as she stood, shaking uncontrollably, shock beyond words. Without speaking he carried to the nurse's office, kicking the door open with his foot.

The nurse stood, shocked, then cleared the gurney for Attico to set Temple down on the bed. "What happened?"

"Brett Forrester tried to rape her," Attico said, his anger a roiling, fiery thing. He swept his hand over Temple's forehead as she started to process what just happened.

"Sweetheart? Temple?" The nurse, Joan, took her hand. "Darling, do you want me to call the police?"

"Yes." Attico.

"No." Temple found her voice at last. She was leaning against Attico, his hard body a comfort to her frayed nerves. "I'm okay. Please, I don't want the police here."

Attico, to his credit, didn't contradict her, but his mouth set in a hard line. "He hit her."

"My jaw does hurt a little." *A lot.*

Joan nodded. "I'll get you some painkillers and some ice. Wait here."

When they were alone, she looked up at Attico. "That's the second time you've saved me from Brett. What are you doing here? I thought I was meeting you in Paris."

He cupped her face with his big hand. "I couldn't wait. I flew in an hour ago and I was going to call you, surprise you. I don't know what made me come here first ... I was hoping to see you in person. Not like *that*, though. Are you sure you're okay?"

"I'm fine, just a little shook up."

His thumb was stroking her cheek, and it felt so good, Temple closed her eyes and leaned into it. She felt him slide his other hand into her hair. She opened her eyes, looking up at him—God, he was beautiful—and then he bent his head and brushed his lips against hers.

So, so sweet and all too brief. Joan came back then and Temple had no time to process her feelings. "Here you go, sweetheart. Just hold it against your jaw; hopefully it'll lessen the bruising." Joan handed her the ice pack and some aspirin. Temple threw them back and held the pack against her face.

Joan smiled at her. "Okay?"

"I'm fine."

Joan cut her eyes at Attico and mouthed *"Wow"* at Temple behind his back. It cheered Temple up and she giggled. Joan made a shushing motion at her. "Well, if you two are okay here?"

"We're fine, thank you, Joanie."

"You're welcome, darling." She looked at Attico. "Look after this one, sir. She's very precious to us all."

Attico smiled at the nurse. "Me too. Thank you again."

WHEN THEY WERE ALONE AGAIN, Attico offered Temple his hand. "Can I drive you home?"

She nodded. "I have my Bug here."

"I can drive it, no problems."

Temple grinned at him. "This I have to see."

Despite her teasing, he drove her ancient car well back to her apartment, and she invited him in.

"Are you sure? I don't want to ..."

"Fibonacci, get your sweet ass up the stairs," she said, laughing. "I have a fridge full of beer and a sofa for two. Sound good?"

"Sounds perfect."

. . .

ATTICO WATCHED as she moved around her tiny kitchen, gathering chips and beer, and helped her out when her hands were too full. They camped out on her sofa and talked, finding it surprisingly easy not to talk about what had happened tonight. He sensed she just wanted to forget it, and he respected that. He wouldn't forget. He would make Brett Forrester pay if it was the last thing he did.

But for tonight, he kept the tone light. Dressed in just a T-shirt and a knee-length skirt, she looked younger than her years, her dark hair falling loosely about her shoulders. A bruise was forming on her jaw and he couldn't help but reach out and stroke it. "Does it hurt?"

She shook her head, gazing at him. He smiled and leaned over to kiss her. Her lips opened as they met his and they embraced, deeply, slowly, his tongue caressing hers. God, she tasted so sweet.

"Attico?"

He couldn't stop touching her beautiful face. "Yes?"

"I ... um ... I don't know if ... I'm not ready for ..."

He smiled. "Temple, I meant it when I said I wasn't expecting anything. What is it *you* want?"

She hesitated for a long time. "You. I *do* want you, Attico, I swear I do. I just ... I haven't ..."

Attico got it suddenly. "Oh. Wow."

Temple bit her lip. "Yeah ... I know it's crazy but I just never wanted to before."

He smiled, stroking her cheek. "Like I said, nothing needs to happen until you want it to. If you ever want it to."

"Don't say that ... I *do* want you, Attico. I can't stop thinking about you, it's just—"

"—it's okay, sweetheart. Let's get to know each other."

He wrapped his arm around her shoulder, drawing her close, and she snuggled into him, her head on his chest. "Will you think it strange if I ask you to stay tonight?"

He adored the way her voice shook, so unsure of him, of herself. "I'd be honored. I can sleep on the couch, no problem."

Temple nodded, then looked up with him and gave the briefest shake of her head. "No ... would you lie down with me?"

He pressed his lips to hers. "I would love to."

TEMPLE WONDERED if she was being a tease, asking him to lay with her, but she needed his presence, his arms around her. Brett's attack had shaken her more than she was admitting to Attico and she needed someone—no, she needed *him*—to be with her tonight.

In the bedroom, she shyly took off her T-shirt and skirt as he pulled his sweater over his head. God, he was magnificent, broad shouldered, well-defined muscles, flat stomach. She felt her face flame red when she saw him notice her admiration. Attico came to her, sliding his arms around her waist, drawing her close. He was so tall that her breasts pressed against his stomach. She couldn't help but feel small and precious in his arms.

"You're so beautiful," he said softly and bent his head to kiss her.

Temple felt his erection through his underpants and he smiled ruefully. "Sorry. It's out of my control when I'm in your company."

She giggled, grateful that he made what could have been an awkward moment so comfortable. They laid down together on her bed, Attico drawing her close, wrapping his thickly muscled arms around her. He tilted her face up so he could kiss her. "I'm glad I came back."

"So am I, for more reasons than just Brett Forrester," she said with a smile. "I've been thinking about you since the night we met."

"Same here." He stroked her cheek with the tip of his finger. "We have plenty of time to get to know each other."

"We do?"

He grinned. "Call me impetuous, but my business means I can work from anywhere in the world. And at the moment, it suits me to work here, in Geneva. I really would like to get to know you, Temple Dubois."

She didn't know when they fell asleep in the end, talking long into the night. All she knew was that when she woke in the morning, still wrapped in his arms, for the first time in a long time, she felt content.

CHAPTER SIX

P*aris*

TEMPLE GAZED out of the jet's window as Paris came into view below them. "Wow. Wow."

Attico, his fingers linked with hers, grinned at her. "First time in Paris?"

Temple nodded. "First time out of Switzerland."

Attico looked surprised. "Really?"

"Really." She grinned at him. "You're wondering about my accent?"

"I am."

Temple laughed. "I grew up around American accents all my life. My parents were American."

"What happened to them?"

"Car wreck. My older sister died too. Out on a mountain pass coming back from a concert."

"I'm sorry."

She smiled but said nothing else just gazed out of the window. "It's so beautiful."

"I agree." But he was looking at her, and the look in his eyes made her entire body flush with desire. Attico brushed his lips against hers. "But it's nothing to the view I have right here."

She gave a moan of desire and pulled his lips back to hers. They didn't even notice when the plane landed, so involved in their embrace were they. Only when an embarrassed pilot came to find them, giving a cough, did they break away from each other.

ATTICO HIMSELF DROVE them into the center of Paris himself and to the George V hotel. Temple had never seen anything like it—even the Academy paled next to its opulence. Attico had indeed booked her a separate room, but she was relieved that it was adjoining his. Even if they didn't make love, she wanted to be close to him.

And even though it scared her, the longer she spent in his company, the more her body was crying out to her that Attico was the one, the one she wanted for her first … her last? He was so funny, goofy, charming … so devastatingly sexy. When she'd woken up, just before him this morning, she had felt his cock, hard, thick, and long against her thigh and all she could think about was it being inside her. Checking he was asleep, she had gently run her fingertips down the length of it, feeling it twitch, stiffen. He was huge, and she wondered if she, a virgin, could even cope with the size of him …

She shivered now at the thought of it but it wasn't a shiver of fright. Her entire body felt like electricity pulsed over her skin when he was near and when he looked at her, his green eyes intense on hers, she wanted to be naked with him, making love.

"Are you okay?"

They were in the elevator to their floor and Attico was smiling down at her. She looked up at him with shining eyes, hoping he could see the desire in them. "More than okay."

He touched a finger to her cheek and then they were walking to her suite. As Attico opened the door for her, and stood back to let her in, she gasped at the beauty of the place.

"I'm just next door ..."

She turned to him. "This is beautiful, Attico ... but it ... it seems a waste to have two rooms." She flushed bright red, but he smiled.

"Then, let's just think of the suite next door as ... a bolt hole. Just in case."

He drew her into his arms and kissed her. "Do you want to nap before we go out?"

Suddenly she wasn't tired at all. She looked up at him through her long eyelashes and shook her head slowly. "No, I'm not tired ... Attico."

Tentatively she slid her hand down to his groin, feeling his cock respond immediately. His eyes were serious on hers. "Are you sure?"

She nodded, not trusting herself to speak. He stroked her face. "We'll take it slow, darling. I promise I won't hurt you ... and if at any time, you want to stop or you get scared, we stop, okay? Promise me you'll tell me if you get scared."

"I promise." Her voice was gravelly as he led her to the vast bed. He kissed her then leaned his forehead against hers.

"I'm going to get you so wet, Temple, that you'll only feel pleasure ..." He began to unbutton the light cotton dress she was wearing, pushing from her shoulders so she stood only in her bra and panties. He ran a leisurely hand over her belly. "You're heavenly. Lay down for me, baby."

Temple let him take the lead as he covered her body with his, tugging his own shirt off as he did. He kissed her mouth, trailed his lips along her jawline, pressed them against the hollow at the base of her throat.

Temple gasped as he pulled a cup of her bra down and took her nipple into his mouth. His tongue flicked around her nipple as his hand slid into her panties and began to stroke her clit. Sweet sensations flooded her body and her hands, seemingly of their own accord, were on his chest, stroking, feeling the hard muscles contract beneath her touch.

Attico sucked on both of her nipples until they were rock-hard and uber-sensitive, then his lips were on her belly, his tongue circling her navel, dipping deep into it until it quivered with desire.

Temple felt her sex flood with damp warmth as he stroked her almost to the point of orgasm. "Please," she whispered urgently, "I want to cum for the first time with you inside me."

Attico sat back on his haunches, plucking a condom from his jeans as he pushed them down and freed his rampant cock from his underwear. Temple watched as he rolled the condom down the length of it and hitched her legs around his waist. "Slowly," he promised, and she nodded, barely able to wait now.

The moment his cock nudged at her, there was a moment of panic but then with one long, slow stroke he was inside her and Temple cried out, pleasure and pain mingling. They made love slowly, kissing, building the tension between them until Temple felt an explosion of ecstasy through her body and she shivered and trembled as she came, Attico's mouth on hers.

Afterward, he lay next to her, stroking her belly as she caught her breath. "Are you all right?"

Temple gave a breathless chuckle. "More than."

He traced the line of her stomach down to her navel. "Your body is incredible."

"Ha. Thank you. I could do with losing a couple of pounds."

"Nonsense." He kissed her. "Don't change a thing, you're perfect."

She cupped his cheek with her hand. "You're the one who is perfect. When is the other shoe going to drop?"

He frowned a little. "What do you mean?"

She chuckled to show him she was kidding. "White knight, generous to a fault, an incredible lover. What's the catch?"

"Ha, I'm not perfect by any means and I'm sure you'll find that out. But, the thing is, Temple ... I want to be. I want to be perfect for as long as I can be for you. I would never want to let you down."

"We have plenty of time to worry about making mistakes. And we will. I know I will." She grinned at him. "Until then ... can we do that again?"

And she laughed as Attico, grinning triumphantly, covered her body with his and they began again.

"GOD, how am I supposed to concentrate on this exhibit with you in that dress?" Attico murmured to her as she handed him her coat and twirled so he could see her. A midnight blue, beaded dress, backless, and some light gold jewelry that made her skin glow, and her hair swept up into a messy side bun.

"You are glorious," he said, "And I'll show you just how glorious when we get back to the hotel tonight."

Temple grinned at him. Her thighs ached, her sex was throbbing after they had made love for most of the afternoon, and she was still on an endorphin high from it. Her fingers were linked with his and there was a new closeness there, as if they both shared a secret. Which she guessed they did. Every time he touched her, she felt exhilarated, as if she would scream her delight out.

Attico, too, seemed buoyed up, grinning, joking around. It made her glad to see the sadness she had seen in his eyes the first time they had met had gone. She couldn't quite believe it was her that was making him so happy.

"Come meet Maceo," he said and led her across the gallery to an incredible handsome man, who greeted them with a smile. Attico introduced her to Maceo Bartoli, who in turn called his wife Ori over to meet them.

Temple felt shy around all these accomplished people and for a moment, wanted to run and hide in the bathroom. But both Maceo and Ori were incredibly friendly, and they led both Attico and Temple around the exhibit.

"I hope you're going to be buying," Maceo told Attico with a grin and Attico laughed.

"As a matter of fact, I am looking. I might be building a new hotel soon, at least, that's the plan."

"Where?"

Attico grinned at Temple. "Geneva. Perhaps on the Lake."

"Lovely. Come, let's get your drinks refilled and then we can bitch about all the art critics."

TEMPLE EXCUSED herself to use the bathroom and as she returned, she was stopped by a man. "Hi," he said with a friendly smile. "I saw you come in with Attico Fibonacci."

She nodded, a little wary.

"We're old friends from New York. Excuse my manners, Denny Fleet." He held out his hand, and she shook it.

"Temple Dubois."

"Wonderful to meet you. I had no idea Attico had such a lovely partner. Yes, wonderful to meet you. Ah, I see Attico is looking for you, I won't keep you."

Okay, this guy was a little weird. Temple smiled politely and moved away, meaning to ask Attico about him, but then Attico was introducing her to some more friends and she forgot all about the strange man.

THE EVENING PASSED in a flurry of chat, drinks, and exquisite art and it was after midnight when Attico and Temple took a cab back to their hotel. Halfway back, Attico asked the cab driver to take them to the Eiffel Tower first. They stepped out under the Tower, lit up and sparkling in the night sky.

Temple felt tears spring into her eyes. This was all such a dream —the city, the Tower—the man who was holding her hand right now. She shook her head and laughed and told him what she was thinking.

"It's not a dream," he said gently. "This is just the beginning. We are going to have such a happy life, Temple. I know it in my marrow. We were meant to meet."

And looking up at him, Temple knew he was speaking the absolute truth.

CHAPTER SEVEN

G *eneva*

"WHY DO YOU LOOK SO GLOWY?" Zella asked Temple three days later as they made their way to the exhibition school. "Did you get laid?"

Temple snorted with laughter. "I'm absolutely sure you've just broken every rule of the school by asking me that."

"Meh, I've graduated. They can't take it away now. Well? And don't lie because we've all seen that gorgeous tall drink of water driving you to the school every morning. Although it's mean of you to make him drive that junkyard of yours."

"Hey, Delilah is my faithful Bug. Do not speak ill of her."

"She's avoiding the question." Grey came up behind them. He nudged Zella. "And you're useless at getting information. Come on, Tem, spill it."

"Not a chance. Come on, let's get to work. Everyone here?"

. . .

THEY SPENT the morning discussing each of the artifacts in turn. Temple had decided to leave the discussion of the tarot deck until the last week because there was so much to say. Still, both she and her students couldn't help going back to study the horrific cards.

"What I don't get," Rosario said one afternoon, "is what purpose would they serve like this? No one is going to ask for a reading from something like this unless they want to know how they're going to die."

"Well, technically speaking, during a reading, the images don't really have that much to do with the meaning of the cards. The Fool, for example, well, his meaning is the same whether it's this deck or the *Hanson Roberts* or the *Witches* tarot."

"And they were found here in the Academy?"

Temple nodded. "Twenty-something years ago. The contractors found them after the demolition of a wall, perfectly preserved in an old tin. Rumor is, however, that they were placed there *after* the wall was demolished."

She let that piece of information sink in. "You mean ... someone put it there to make it seem like it had been buried for years?"

Temple nodded. "That's just my theory."

"Because of the murder?"

Temple took a deep breath in and nodded. They all knew who her brother was, where he was now, what had happened. "Obviously, we can't discuss this within the remit of the class because I could be —and I am—biased."

"For what it's worth, none of us believe your brother had anything to do with it."

Temple smiled at Zella now. "Zella, you weren't even born when it happened. How do you know?"

"Because no one who shares your DNA could be responsible for a murder. It's just not an option."

There were murmurs of assent from the rest of the class and Temple felt her eyes fill with tears. "Thank you," she said, her voice breaking. "Thank you all for that."

.   .   .

SHE TOLD Attico when he came to pick her up and he smiled at her. "I agree with them. Are the cards that bad?"

Temple nodded. "Come and see."

She took him to the exhibition, and they studied the cards together. "Christ," Attico said, shaking his head, but there was something else in his eyes that she didn't understand.

"What?"

"I hate the idea of you being around these things," he said. "They radiate evil."

She nodded. "I can't argue with that." She touched the glass above one of the Major Arcana. "This one haunts me."

Attico looked at the card. Temple nodded at it. "Judgement. Usually depicting the angel Metatron, at least we think it's Metatron, overseeing the dead rising from the grave. But this one, the weeping woman standing over a young girl with her throat cut. It's so malevolent. As if the card is judging the woman for not saving the other woman in time. As if to say 'there is no protection from evil.' *God.*" She shivered and Attico put his arm around her.

"Come away now, Tem. You've spent enough time with these things for one day."

He DROVE her back to her apartment. He was staying there now, with her, and it was strange but after a day, it felt like he was meant to be there. "I'm sure your Manhattan apartment is seventeen times the size of this place and with a better view."

"Hey, believe it or not, I'm a simple guy and this place is just adorable. And I have the best view right here."

He snaked his arms around her waist and she giggled. "Cheesy."

"You bet." He glanced at his watch. "Listen, I hate to do this but I need to make a couple of calls to New York. Make sure Tony isn't running my company into the ground."

"Go right ahead. I'll make us some supper. Pasta okay with you?" She grinned when she realized she was asking an Italian if he liked pasta. "Never mind."

As she boiled water for the pasta and chopped up garlic, onions, and tomatoes for the sauce, she pondered how natural this seemed, when she'd barely known anything like this before. A family meal. She had grown so used to eating in the school's cafeteria for most of her life, that even when she had first moved into this apartment, she had lived on cereal, not bothering to cook just for one.

But having Attico here, she got to play chef, digging out her mother's old recipe books to try to find something that would suit his refined tastes. Attico, however, seemed happy with whatever she made—so far, at least.

They'd flown back from Paris together after a blissful weekend of sightseeing and lovemaking and now Temple could barely remember a time when she hadn't known this man. Everything about him was just ... right.

"You're grinning like a loon," he said now, coming into the room, shoving his phone back into the pocket of his jeans. He kissed her neck, then pretended to bite it, making her giggle.

"Because of the loon I have right here," she said. She turned in his arms and kissed him. "And I hope you're hungry because I overestimated the pasta and now there's enough for a small army."

"You know me. I'll finish it."

But when she laid the dish in front of him, he did pale a little. "You weren't exaggerating."

Temple laughed. "Nope. But the joy of pasta is that you can have it as leftovers, so don't worry about finishing it."

"Gah, cold pasta?" He made a face, and she grinned.

"Ah, so I learned something new. Cold pasta, huh?"

"And ... and don't tell anyone back in the States this, but peanut butter and jelly. Nope."

Temple pretended to gape at him. "You sure they'll let you back in the country?"

"Not if they find out. How about you, any weird food things?"

Temple considered. "There's a French sausage called Andouillette. Made from chitterlings." She made a gagging noise.

"Enough said." Attico looked vaguely horrified, then laughed. "So noted, not keen on French sausage ..."

"Italian sausage, though ..." They both snorted and Attico shook his head.

"Why is it I feel like a teenager around you?"

Temple kept her face blank. "Can you remember being one? Really?"

"Oh *burn*." Attico cackled with laughter, his eyes crinkling as he chuckled. "Listen, young 'un, now that you mention it ... this old man need a hand to get up and into bed."

"Oh really?" Temple shrieked with laughter as he pulled her onto his lap. She snaked her hand down to his groin and squeezed his cock. "Hmm, seems to me this old man has no trouble getting *up*."

"I've corrupted you," Attico mock-groaned. "In less than a week, I've corrupted you."

"I know, well done, Mr. Fibonacci." Temple kissed him, giggling. "Consider me corrupted, and willing to be even more corrupted."

"Is that so? Well, in that case, maybe we don't even need to get to the bedroom."

In a flash he had her on the floor of the living room, showering kisses on her, blowing raspberries on her skin until she was crying with laughter. He stripped her slowly and hooked her legs over his shoulders. "Lay back, beautiful," he said, grinning up at her. "I'm going to make you cum so hard that they'll hear you scream in Austria."

Temple sighed happily and did as he asked, gasping and moaning as his tongue lashed around her clit. She was almost at her peak when her cell phone rang.

"Ignore it," came the command from between her thighs, and she gasped her agreement.

It was only when the phone kept ringing that she sat up. "I'm sorry, honey, I have to get that. It might be Luc."

Attico sat up, sighing. "Of course. Please, go ahead."

Temple shot him an apologetic glance as she grabbed her phone from her purse on the sofa. "Sorry, baby." She looked at the screen. "Damn, it *is* the facility."

She answered the call and a familiar voice greeted her. It was Luc's designated nurse. "Temple, I'm so sorry to disturb you but it ... it's Luc."

Even before she said the words, Temple knew what she would say. Her beloved, broken brother was gone

Luc was dead.

CHAPTER EIGHT

Temple's eyes felt like they had sand in them. As the doctors talked to her, she listened but didn't take anything in. Luc was dead. Her last family member was gone. They told her that the nurses had found him dead in bed during the final checks of the night.

"His body just gave up," they told her, but Temple couldn't believe it. For all his problems, Luc had been healthy and vital, even if his brain was damaged. There had been no signs he was sick.

She felt Attico's arms around her. "Sweetheart, I'm going to take you home now."

"I don't want to leave Luc alone."

Attico's lips pressed against her temple. "They're taking him to the medical examiner's office, baby. We can't stay with him there, but I promise, I'll take you there first thing in the morning."

On the drive back to her apartment, Attico held her hand. "I'm so sorry, darling. I can't imagine."

"He was only your age, Attico. And despite everything ... he seemed to be doing really well. I can't believe it."

Her voice broke, and she began to cry softly. Attico pulled the car over and drew her into his arms. "Baby ..."

Temple didn't know how long they sat there but eventually they got back to her apartment. Attico made her drink some hot tea and put her to bed. She held out her hand to him. "I need you next to me."

"Give me five minutes to make some calls, baby, and I'm all yours."

She didn't argue with him, just nodded and closed her eyes. She was asleep even before he left the room.

ATTICO CLOSED the bedroom door quietly and went into the living room, dialing Tony's number. He told his brother what had happened.

"Christ, poor kid." Tony was sympathetic.

"I know. Look, I don't know why but something is hinky about Luc Monfils' death."

"Why do you say that?"

Attico sighed. "It came out of nowhere, Tony. Even with his problems, he was a pretty healthy guy."

"Wasn't he pretty much a vegetable?"

Attico was silent and Tony cursed softly. "Sorry, that was in poor taste. Look ... after everything that happened ..."

"That's the thing, Tony. It's too coincidental. Tony ... the tarot deck is back at the Academy."

This time Tony really was stunned into silence. "Are they fucking insane?"

"They don't *know*, Tony. They don't know its history. They think it was found in the school, but they have no idea about Winter Blood. It was covered up pretty good, by the sounds of it."

"Shit, Atti. The last thing we need is all that shit coming out. I hate to say it but maybe Monfils dying was for the best."

"Don't say that. Temple's alone because he died."

"You're right. Sorry. But Atti, just remember, you did nothing wrong."

"You know that's not true."

"You had nothing to do with that society, Atti. And how the hell were you to know how fucking sick its former members were?"

"The girl died."

"Did you kill her? No. You were a kid, Atti. A *kid*."

AFTER HE HUNG UP, Attico sat in the living room. *Fuck.* Now Luc had died, his death would be reported in the press, and all the crap from before would be dragged up. Temple would know that he, Attico, knew more about what happened to her brother than he'd told her. Not a great way to build trust in their relationship.

Attico still remembered that terrible night when the young woman had been murdered. He had been the one to find her body, tied to a lamppost on the Academy ground. She had been stabbed to death, run through with a sword stolen from the museum. The way she had been dressed, in a medieval-type gown, blindfolded ... the scene was copied directly from one of the Winter Blood tarot cards. He'd been the one to turn in her killer.

Attico himself had been questioned by police, but then his father had swept in and Attico had been spirited back to the States. He knew he had nothing to do with the death, but it didn't make him feel any better. The tie-in with the Winter Blood Tarot was linked to the society at the Academy. He'd been aware that some of his cohort were fascinated by the recent finding, but not that they had bought into its horrific, deadly ideology.

And now it had been returned to the Academy, and now Luc Monfils was dead and with him, possibly the last link to why the girl had been killed, except Atti himself. *Damn it.* He knew he shouldn't have started this thing with Temple, but he couldn't help himself. He'd thought about her every moment and in the end, he'd had to fly back to Geneva to find her.

Thank God he had because otherwise Brett Forrester would have raped her and Temple would have been destroyed. *God.* She hadn't called the police, but he'd insisted she go to the dean. Brett Forrester had been removed from the school immediately and Attico had stupidly assumed all their problems would be over now.

That damn card deck ...

"Atti?"

He heard her soft voice from the bedroom and, leaving his phone in the living room, went to her. Temple was sitting up in bed, still looking dazed, mussed up from sleep but she reached out to him and he went to her.

His lips were soft against hers. "Sweetheart ... how are you?"

"Numb."

Attico wrapped his arms around her, pressing his lips to her forehead. "I'm so sorry about Luc, Temple. I would give anything to bring him back for you."

"I'm just grateful his passing was peaceful," Temple mumbled, her face pressed to his chest, "and that you're here." She looked up at him. "I have no right to expect your support after this short a time and if this is too heavy for you ..."

"Hush," Attico smiled down at her, stroking her cheek. "This is you and me from now on, okay? We take things day by day, but I'm in this."

He felt her body relax against him. "I know this may seem strange on such a night ... but I need to be close to you." Her voice shook, still nervous. "Will you make love to me?"

His lips were firm against hers before she'd even finished her sentence. Slowly they undressed and Attico gathered to him. "Sweet Temple ... you make my heart sing."

She had tears in her eyes but she didn't speak, just nodded, and they began to make love, taking their time, enjoying every sensation, every touch.

His fingers trailed lightly down her body, stroking the soft curve of her belly before dipping between her legs to caress her clit with his thumb. He slid two fingers inside her, feeling her damp warmth as his tongue explored her mouth.

Her hands were on his cock, stroking, teasing it until it was so hard it was almost painful. Temple rolled the condom down the thick length of it and Attico hitched her legs around his hips.

He teased her by pushing in only a couple of inches then withdrawing, grinning at her moan of frustration, before, with one long, hard thrust, burying his cock deep inside her velvety cunt. God, she was so tight, but despite her inexperience, she knew what to do to please him, constricting her vaginal muscles around him, squeezing her thighs against his hips, tilting them up to meet him. "Christ, Temple, you're so fucking beautiful ..."

His coarse language seemed to ignite something in her and their lovemaking became rough, almost feral in their need for each other. Attico pinned her hands to the bed with his own, gazing down at her, his brow furrowed as he slammed his cock deeper and harder into her. Temple arched her back up, gasping and panting, completely in the moment with him.

He watched her face as she came, marveling over the rose-pink flush in her cheeks, the sheen of dewy sweat on her dusky skin. Attico reached his own peak, groaning, burying his face in her neck as he panted for breath.

They collapsed back on the bed, breathless and trembling, kissing, their gaze never leaving the others. Attico knew he was in trouble. This girl ... she was intoxicating. He cupped her sweet face in his hands. "I'm crazy about you, Temple Dubois."

"And I you, Attico. Very much."

And for the rest of the night, they showed each other how much they cared, over and over.

CHAPTER NINE

T emple read through the autopsy report again and again but the reality still didn't sink it. *Cause of Death ... Asphyxiation.* Luc had been *murdered.*

Temple turned and threw up in the medical examiner's trash can. Both he and Attico steered her back into her chair and Temple put her head in her hands. "I don't believe it."

"I'm so sorry, Mademoiselle Dubois, but there was no doubt in my mind or my colleagues. We have to involve the police now, of course."

Temple nodded. "Of course."

The medical examiner looked at Attico. "I'll give you some privacy."

"Thank you, Doctor."

Temple looked up at Attico. "There's only one person who would do this."

"Forrester."

She nodded. "He's the only one with a motive."

Attico sat down beside her. "I hate to say this but ... what about the family of the girl Luc was suspected of killing?"

Temple shook her head. "She was never identified. And after all this time? They had over twenty years to come for him." She sighed, leaning into Attico's arms. "No, it has to be Brett. Twisted fucker."

BUT WHEN THE police questioned Brett Forrester, he had a rock-solid alibi. "I was in Vienna," he told them snootily, "with about three hundred witnesses. I was speaking at a conference for two days. I'll give you a list of attendees."

The police told Temple, and she was at a loss. Attico noticed the chief of police watching Temple's reactions carefully. With a jolt, he realized that Temple, too, was a suspect and when the police chief had let them alone, he broached the subject gently.

"Sweetheart, there's a chance you could be questioned too."

Temple blinked. "What?"

"There's no need to worry. You have an alibi too—me. I'm just saying, the police will explore every avenue."

Temple blew out her cheeks. "Jesus."

"I know. But they have to look at everything in a murder."

She nodded, looking exhausted. Attico kissed her. "Darling, I really think I should take you away. Come back to the States with me for a while."

She shook her head. "Thank you, but I can't. I have to arrange Luc's funeral and I still have a commitment to the school for the summer. I won't let my students down."

HER STUDENTS HAD HEARD, of course, and when she walked into the classroom, she saw the huge arrangement of flowers and nearly broke down. For a moment, she didn't know what to say, but in the end, she nodded, tried to smile, and said thank you in a broken voice.

Grey stuck his hand in the air. "Temple, can we talk about the tarot today?"

Temple was grateful that her students sensed she didn't want to talk about Luc and nodded gratefully. "No problem. Shall we go over what we already know, then discuss each card? Obviously, we won't get to the whole deck, so let's concentrate on the Major Arcana, okay?"

The students murmured in assent, and Temple cued up the projection screen, flicking to an overview of the picture cards of the tarot deck. She ran through the age, the history, the materials used to create the cards, then gave the students a quick pop quiz on the history of tarot, firing off questions to each student. She smiled at them. "Great, you really know your stuff. Okay." She huffed out her cheeks. "Let's start on one of the less violent cards, if there is such a thing." She cued up a single card on the screen. "The Empress. Anyone tell me what she signifies?"

Barry put his hand up. "Femininity, beauty, Mother Nature, that kind of thing."

"Spot on. And in reverse?"

"Hidden agendas, two-faced?"

"Hmm. That's more the High Priestess' reverse meaning. Olivia?"

Olivia, a sweet-faced English girl, smiled. "I think the Empress' reverse is something like writer's block?"

"That's right, a creative block, and an overreliance on others. Right, so usually the Empress is depicted on her throne, with the scepter in her hand representing life, the twelve stars on her crown depicting her control of her year, surrounded by abundant crops. Now, in this deck, The Empress is depicted as a demon, the scepter a severed limb, and the crops here are instead a sea of blood. She still wears a crown, but instead of stars, plucked out eyeballs." Temple studied the card. "And yet this is one of the tamer cards. Delightful."

The class snickered a little at her sarcastic tone and she grinned sheepishly. "Okay, so there are no right and wrong answers. There's no guidebook with this particular tarot, so let's discuss why we think the artist decided to depict her like this."

For the next hour and a half, the class debated, argued, and laughed, discussing the card, and Temple was distracted from her grief. At the end, Zella came up and hugged her. "I'm so sorry, Temple."

Temple thanked her and the others for their kindness and the flowers and carried the arrangement back to her office. She was marking up some papers when there was a knock at the door. "Come in, please."

The chief of police, Renard, entered, giving her a reserved smile. Temple stood and shook his hand. "How can I help you?"

"Mademoiselle Dubois, I'm here to ask you to accompany me to the station for questioning in the death of your brother."

Even though she had been expecting it, it was still a shock but Temple nodded. "Of course."

Luckily, most of the rest of the school was in class as she followed the police officer to his car. To her relief, he didn't make her sit in the back like a perp and she thanked him for his consideration.

He smiled. "Mademoiselle, you are not under arrest. It's just with any murder, we have to interview everyone and anyone."

"Of course. I'll tell you everything I know, but I have to tell you, with Brett Forrester cleared, I have little idea who might have done this and why."

"Well, it's my job to find that out but anything you can tell us might be of help."

WHILE CHIEF RENARD was courteous and sympathetic, his colleague, Hubert, was anything but and Temple realized they were playing good cop/bad cop with her. While Renard kept his questions to her relationship with her brother, Hubert grilled her about her relationship with Attico Fibonacci.

"Would you say, Mademoiselle Dubois, that the only thing keeping you from pursuing your relationship with Mr. Fibonacci in the United States was that your brother tied you to Geneva?"

Temple swallowed the biting retort she had in her mind and shook her head. "My brother was never a burden, sir. *Never.* He was my only blood family."

"But he did tie you to Geneva."

"The facility he lived in is a kind, compassionate one. If I had wished to travel to the States, there would not have been a problem.

As you well know by now, Mr. Fibonacci is currently working from Geneva."

"But that can't continue, can it? And, forgive me, but looking at your financial records, you can hardly afford to keep flying back and forth. But perhaps, with Mr. Fibonacci's money that's not an issue."

Temple's eyes narrowed, but she refused to rise to the bait. "I believe I have stated my case, M. Hubert. I loved my brother dearly. Not only that, but I have a solid alibi for the night he was killed."

Hubert's smile was chilly. "Perhaps someone was paid to end your brother's life and therefore free you to travel with your paramour."

Bastard. He was going to go after Attico, that's what he was saying. "As I have told you, I had no need to be 'freed' by anything nor anyone. Neither I nor Mr. Fibonacci had any reason to kill my brother."

"But you are each other's alibi."

"Yes. And my students, plus the security at the school who saw us leave together that night. I'm sure if you check the security cameras at my apartment building, you can see us entering the building just after seven and not leaving again until we received the call from the facility later that night."

Hubert didn't have an answer for that, of course, and the rest of the interview passed without any snark from the older man. Nevertheless, Temple was relieved when it was over.

Hubert insisted on showing her out though and couldn't resist one last shot. "I had a very interesting talk with Professor Forrester," he said, his tone sneering. "Apparently the two of you were close."

Temple had had enough now. "If by close you mean he attempted to rape me, then yes. Myself, I don't see that as 'closeness,' more as sexual assault, but hey, that's just me."

She let the door close on Hubert's smug face and stomped out onto the street. She was too pissed to call a cab and instead walked through the city, not making eye contact with anyone, her anger fueling her pace.

It wasn't until she had reached a part of the city where she knew there were a few coffee bars that she slowed down. She chose one randomly then went in and ordered an espresso and a latte, downing the first at the counter, then taking the latte and finding an armchair in which to sink.

She rubbed her face, trying to feel anything but numb. She could only be thankful both for Attico and her students. Without them in her life right now, she could so easily fall apart. Being the summer, a lot of her friends from the school were taking a vacation, even Nicolai, and on other summers she had felt isolated and alone at this time.

Except for Luc. Others might see someone in his position as a burden but Temple never did. Luc was her blood, her brother, and she loved every moment she spent with him. He might not recognize her as his sister, but he knew she loved him as he loved her.

She hated to think of him being frightened, or terrified. They had told her it was entirely possible that he had been asleep when he was smothered, that there didn't appear to be any signs of a struggle, and Temple prayed that had been the case. *God.* She felt sick to her stomach. She closed her eyes and took a few deep breaths. *Oh Luc ... I miss you so much.*

She felt a rush of gratitude that Attico had known her brother, albeit briefly, before his accident, that she had someone to talk to about Luc. Last night, they had ordered in pizza and sat up talking most of the night—well, she had done most of the talking, telling Attico all about her life, her family, what she remembered of them. It had brought them even closer together, and she wished she could take Attico up on his offer to go to the States.

But she still had her class to teach for the next three weeks, then she could think about spending time with him in America before the new school year began. She sipped her latte and scrolled through the messages on her phone. Three were from Attico, asking if she was okay, and she texted him back, telling him she was fine and would be home soon.

Another was from Zella. *If you need someone to talk to ...*

That was typical Zella. Temple smiled and send her student a thank-you message.

The last message was a photo. It was one of the cards of the tarot deck and came with no message. Temple frowned as she opened the image and saw the card for "Judgement," the one she had pointed out to Attico. The woman weeping over the body of the murdered girl. Temple checked the number the text had come from. *Unknown.*

Weird. She ruminated on it for a while then brushed it aside. She had better things to do, like arranging Luc's funeral.

She finished her coffee and walked out into a steady rain but ignored it and walked home. The apartment was quiet, and she found a note from Attico on the table.

BABY,

Viewing some potential office spaces in the city this afternoon.

I'll be back before dinner—how does a table at Domaine de Chateau-vieux sound?

Love A x

TEMPLE HALF SMILED. "Expensive. That's how it sounds." Whether she acknowledged Hubert's words, the jibes he'd thrown at her to get a reaction, the less than subtle inference that she was a gold-digger, had stung.

Actually, I'm really tired—can I have a raincheck? I'm sorry. x.

Back came a reply straightaway.

You okay? No problem, of course. I can pick up some takeout on my way back. Love A x

She chuckled a little. She knew who had sent her the text, she thought, but she thought it was cute how he signed his initial, anyway.

Perfect. See you soon. Hope you find somewhere good for your office. x

This time, he replied with a simple 'love heart' emoticon. She grinned and wondered whether the younger realtor had shown him how to send one. "My old man." She smiled and reminded herself to tease him later.

She spent the next couple of hours online, trying to find a funeral

home to help her give Luc the sendoff he deserved. The trouble was
... there was no one apart from her, and now Attico, to attend a
funeral and so she selected a small non-religious service at the home
itself, then cremation. She would ask Attico to come with her into the
mountains to scatter her brother's ashes.

ATTICO, in the meantime, thanked the realtor and got into his car. For
a moment, he hesitated before driving away. The offices he had seen
were nice but Tony had called this afternoon, asking when he would
be home. "Dad's drinking again, Atti. It's bad."

Fuck. Sebastiano's alcoholism had gotten worse since their mother's death but Attico had thought his father had been through
enough rehab that it would stick this time. No such luck.

But he couldn't dream of leaving Geneva right now, not when
Temple was alone.

The fact her brother had been murdered ... he couldn't help
worry that whoever had killed Luc would come after Temple next,
but he knew that was paranoia ... wasn't it?

He jumped as someone banged on his window and he rolled the
window down to see a man smiling at him. "Hey! Attico Fibonacci!
What the hell are you doing here?"

It took Attico a moment to remember the guy. Derry? Derek? The
man laughed. "Denny Fleet. From the gym?"

"Oh, of course, I'm sorry." Attico got out of his car and shook
hands with Denny. "Good to see you again."

Denny grinned, but stayed silent, obviously waiting for Attico to
explain his presence in Switzerland. Attico gave a half smile. "My
partner lives here in Geneva. I'm on my way home now."

"I thought I hadn't seen you at the gym for a while. Not slacking
on the workouts, I hope."

Christ, this guy was a bore. "Not at all. What brings you to
Geneva, Denny?"

"Ah, family. So, you're here with your girlfriend? Oh, sorry, I
shouldn't assume in this day and age. Girlfriend or boyfriend?"

Attico was bemused. "Girlfriend. Temple. Well, Denny, good to see you but I have to get back."

"Matters of the heart, eh? Happens to us all. Good to see you, Fibonacci."

Denny strode off, leaving Attico staring after him. Christ, a bore *and* a weirdo. Attico gave a short laugh, got into his car, and pulled off into traffic.

He called Temple, who sounded as if she had been asleep. "Hey doofus."

Attico grinned when she giggled. "What kind of greeting is that?"

"I think our relationship should be all sex and mockery, what do you say?"

Temple was still laughing. "Oh, you silly man. You do make me happy, though, thank you. I needed it today."

She told him about the police questioning her. "So, in case you were wondering, they all think I'm a gold-digging hussy murderer." She said it lightly but Attico could tell she was upset.

"Assholes. I'll rip them new ones."

"Don't, it's not worth it." He heard her sigh. "Just come home. I'll cook us something. I need you here now."

"On my way, beautiful."

TEMPLE WAS in his arms the moment he stepped through the door. "That's one hell of a greeting."

She pressed her lips to his. "I've been waiting for you." She grabbed his hand and guided it under her robe. Attico grinned when he felt how wet she was.

"God, you shameless little creature."

Temple giggled. "Well, if I'm going to be accused of being a strumpet, I'm damn well going to act like one."

She led him to the bedroom and started to strip him. Attico stroked her face, studying her. "You okay?" She seemed a little strung out and for the first time he wondered if she was taking anything. She'd told him she hadn't wanted any medical help after Luc died but now with his murder ... she didn't seem like his sweet Temple. "Baby, slow down a little." He took hold of her hands and studied her. "Did you take something?"

Temple sighed and shook her head. "No. I swear I didn't. God, Attico ... I think I'm trying to distract myself from wanting to scream, is all. I'm sorry, I didn't mean to freak you out."

Attico smiled. "It's okay. You're not the first one to do that today."

"What?"

"Ah, nothing. Just ran into this strange guy from New York ... doesn't matter. What does matter is you." He kissed her softly. "You hungry?"

"Only for you."

"Tem."

She smiled. "I just want you close, Atti. That's all."

He nodded, and they went to bed but didn't make love. Attico made her tell him all about what the police had told her and asked her, shaking his head when she told him how Hubert's words had affected her. "I should at least make a complaint."

"No, please don't."

He studied her. "You know that's crap, right? If I thought for one second you were with me for my money or security or anything, I wouldn't have started this thing. It's bullshit. You and me, we're endgame, Temple. I know it in my heart."

Her eyes filled with tears and he pressed his lips against her forehead. "You and me, slugger, okay?"

"Okay," she whispered.

Attico drew her into his arms and held her close for the rest of the night.

IN THE MORNING, they awoke to the news that there had been another murder.

CHAPTER TEN

The first person Temple saw was Zella, her face red and puffy from crying, and when she saw her teacher, she ran into Temple's arms. "It's horrible, too horrible, oh God ..."

Temple felt sick. Dean Corke, his elderly eyes watery and shocked, came to her and Attico. He looked like he was about to collapse. Attico steered the old man into a chair. "Dean Corke ... what happened?"

"They found her in the crypt. It hasn't been opened for years, and when the night security checked on why the door was open, they found her." The dean was shaking so much that Attico had to hold his hands.

Chief Renard nodded at them as he came into the dean's office. "I'm so sorry for your loss, but we need someone to identify the body for us."

Temple hugged Zella tightly. "I'll do it."

"Tem, no ..."

"She was my student. It's my responsibility."

. . .

RENARD LED Temple down to the crypt. Before he let her in, he stopped her. His eyes were sympathetic. "It's bad, Mademoiselle Dubois. Prepare yourself." He gave her a second. "Ready?"

She nodded, and he stepped aside. Temple stepped into the crypt and saw a forensics team already working over the prone bod. She walked slowly towards her. "Yes," she said, her voice breaking as she looked down into the sightless eyes of her student, her friend. The gaping wound in her throat. The blood. "Yes, that is Olivia Dolenz. It's Olivia. It's *Olivia* ..."

And Temple began to scream.

THE DOCTOR NODDED AT ATTICO. "I've given her a sedative but she's still awake for now. Still agitated, but she's had the max I can give her. See if you can calm her down. I'm concerned about her blood pressure. If she continues this, we may need to put her out."

Attico nodded. "Cut her a break, doc. Her brother died last week, and now this."

"I'm just concerned. Go in, sit with her. I'm sure that'll help."

Attico walked into the hospital room. Temple was curled up on her side, facing away from him. Attico closed the door to the room, then laid down next to her, spooning into her back, sliding his arm around her waist. "Baby girl."

He felt her sobs even though they were silent and let her cry herself out. His arms tightened around her and he buried his face in her hair. "*Piccolo*, it's okay. I'm here."

Temple's tears shuddered to a halt, and she turned, burying her face in his chest. Attico stroked her hair as he held her, wishing he could take some of her pain away. "I'm so sorry, baby."

She just shook her head, and he knew she was too overwhelmed to speak. Eventually, the sedative kicked in and she slept fitfully, her brow furrowed, her lovely face creased with pain.

Attico waited until he knew she was truly out and slipped from the bed, going into the quiet of the hospital corridor to make a call.

Dean Corke was still awake and when Attico asked him what the school was going to do about the summer classes, the dean was clear.

"We're sending the students home, Mr. Fibonacci, and the school will remain closed for an undetermined period." The elderly man sounded exhausted. "How is Temple?"

"Shell-shocked. Broken. I'm hoping the police will let me take her to the States for a time to recuperate."

"That sounds like a perfect idea." Dean Corke hesitated. "The business with her brother ..."

"She's been cleared, but yes, the police could take her passport." Attico gave a wry smile to himself. "Although I hate to do it, pressure could be brought to bear on them."

"In this circumstance, I don't think anyone would judge you. Temple is simply not capable of hurting anyone—in fact, I would say she herself ... well, perhaps I shouldn't say it."

"Temple might be in danger?" Attico's heart was beating painfully against his ribs.

"Yes. After what happened with Forrester ..."

"I promise you, Dean. No one will hurt Temple."

"Good man. You will send my best wishes to her, tell her that her job is safe for as long as she wants it, would you?"

Attico smiled. "Of course. Thank you, Dean."

TEMPLE WAS STILL SLEEPING as he went back into her room and Attico stroked the hair back from her face. "*Ti amo* ..." he whispered, knowing it to be the truth. In a matter of weeks, he had realized that he had never had what he and Temple had before and that now, he could not imagine his life without her. The thought of someone targeting her, of hurting her, was too much to bear. No. He would take her back to New York for a time, insist on it. He would ask Tony to take over the company full-time for now so he could spend time with her.

He held her hand and sat back in his chair, closing his eyes.

Tomorrow, they would begin to move past this. Tomorrow, they would begin to live again.

DEAN CORKE WAS DRAINED. Eventually the police left the building, having sealed the crypt after Olivia's body was removed. Dean Corke sat down heavily into his chair, feeling every one of his seventy-nine years. Maybe it was time to retire. He rubbed his face and knew he couldn't run away from this situation—it was his responsibility. He had been one of the English tutors back when the girl was killed twenty years ago, and he had been staggered when Luc Monfils was questioned over his involvement. Corke had known that a secret society had been formed, loosely linked to the Winter Blood Tarot, but had assumed it was merely the fascination of the macabre, not actual bloodlust that had fueled the group.

He remembered the Fibonacci brothers had some involvement in the case, too, though he didn't know the extent. Maybe that was why now Attico seemed desperate to prevent anything happening to Temple. He was obviously head over heels for the young teacher and Corke was glad. Temple deserved happiness, especially now.

Dean Corke switched his lamp off and got up to return to his rooms. As he reached the door, he was greeted by a harassed-looking caretaker. "What is it, Joe?"

"Dean Corke ... with everything that went on, I was distracted. I'm so sorry ..."

"What's wrong?"

Joe swallowed nervously. "It's the tarot, Dean. It's missing. It's been stolen."

OLIVIA DOLENZ'S murderer smiled to himself as he used the new burner phone to send the next image of the card to Temple Dubois. She would know, then, what he intended, to recreate the pictures of the Major Arcana, killing people she loved, she cared about, until the final card. *Death.* Hers ...

He looked at the card now, the young maiden, the same woman who had wept over the body of the young woman, now herself dying, a gilded dagger plunged into the center of her. Temple Dubois would suffer the same fate, leaving Attico Fibonacci to find her body and mourn the loss of his love.

Because he had been watching them. Fibonacci was crazy about the young teacher, that much was clear, and she about him. Good.

It would be so much more satisfying when he tore them apart ...

CHAPTER ELEVEN

T o his surprise, Temple didn't argue about him taking her to the States. "But *after* Luc's cremation," she said, and he nodded.

"Of course, my darling one."

Temple had insisted on clearing her departure with the police and, now he learned, she told both Attico and the police about the image of the tarot card that had been texted to her.

"I have no idea who it was from," she said wearily, "and I didn't make any connection to a threat at the time. I wish I had paid more attention ... I might have known someone was in danger."

Chief Renard was sympathetic, and he told Temple she was cleared to leave the country. She gave him a tired half smile. "Does Detective Hubert think so too?"

"He works for me, Mademoiselle Dubois, and he'll have to live with it."

Luc's FUNERAL was held that afternoon, and to Temple's surprise and eternal gratitude, the remaining members of her class attended. She thanked each one of them tearfully. Zella hugged her the hardest. "I'm so sorry, Temple."

"Thank you, honey. Thank you so much." She studied Zella's drawn, wan face. "Are you okay?"

Zella shook her head. "I can't believe she's gone, Tem." Olivia had been Zella's best friend, her roommate. Temple felt tears dropping down her face.

"I know. I can't express the sorrow, the shock. Zella, are your parents coming to pick you up?"

Zella nodded. "But I'm going to wait for Olly's parents. I don't want them here alone."

"I'll be with you for that."

Zella nodded at Attico, who was talking to some of the other students. "He's a good guy. He's taking you back to the States?"

Temple nodded. "For a few weeks. Listen." She dug a card out of her pocket. "The police have my cell phone so I have a new one. Here's the number. If you need to talk, please, call anytime. I mean it. Call anyway, just to check in."

THE DAY they were scheduled to fly back to New York, Temple spent most of the day with Olivia Dolenz's parents. They were understandably shattered and by the time Temple stepped aboard the Fibonacci's jet, she was utterly drained.

As they took off, Attico led her back to the small bedroom at the back of the plane. "I want you to rest, baby."

Temple shook her head. "No, Atti ... I need to be distracted. Please ..."

Attico's lips were against hers then as they stripped each other, then as he laid her down on the bed, he kissed her throat and, moving down, took each nipple into her mouth in turn, sucking on them until they were hard, flicking his tongue around each tiny nub.

Temple sighed and closed her eyes as he moved down her body, his tongue circle her deep navel, his kisses on the soft curve of her belly. When he gently pushed her thighs apart, Temple shivered as his tongue found her clit. All she wanted now was this moment, the electric sensations shooting around her body, every cell soaking up the pleasure, purging the hurt and sorrow of the last few weeks.

She tangled her fingers in Attico's dark curls, pulling on them gently as he teased, licked, and tasted her until she was writhing and panting for air. He brought her to orgasm twice before rolling a condom down his straining cock and thrusting into her.

Temple could hardly believe that she had been a virgin only a few weeks previously. With Attico, she had found her perfect match, physically, sexually, spiritually. The way their bodies fit together so well, despite the height difference between them, was a revelation to her. The way he looked at her, not just her face but her body. He would stroke her belly or slide his hand down the curve of her calf, and his eyes would shine with desire, with arousal.

Even when she was half dressed, hair wet from the shower, Attico's obvious admiration made her feel so sexy that she would do things she had never dreamed she would have the courage to do.

Now, as she gazed up at him, she smiled. God, he was so Goddamn beautiful, those huge green eyes, that crooked smile. "I love you, Attico Fibonacci," she whispered, knowing she meant it with all her heart.

"As I love you, Temple Dubois. So much ... so much ..." Attico's lips were rough against hers. "Temple ... marry me. Be my wife, my partner for all time."

Temple felt a shock run through her. "Attico ... we've only known each other for a few weeks."

"I know, and it's crazy and stupid and reckless but God, who cares? This is it for me, for life. Don't you feel that too?"

Temple smiled at him. "Ask me again when your huge cock isn't buried inside me. My ability to reason is compromised."

Attico chuckled, and they continued to make love, Attico thrusting hard, his cock deeper and harder within her with each moment. His eyes never left hers and Temple dug her nails into his buttocks, urging him on until they both came, moaning and crying out the other's name.

As they caught their breath, Attico ran his hand down her belly. "Marry me," he said again, his eyes shining. "I love you. I've never felt this way about anyone before. I know we still have so much to learn about each other, but let's do it as husband and wife. If you decide to go back to the Academy, I'll move my business wholesale to Geneva."

Temple stroked his face. "What about your family? Won't they have something to say about you marrying a penniless teacher?"

Attico frowned. "You're too hung up on what other people will think."

"I am when it's your family. I would love you whether you were as rich as you are, or as poor as I am. I don't care about money, I never have. But your family could take a very different view and to be honest, I'm not sure I would blame them. They'll want to protect you." She sighed. "Look ... we still have so much to learn about each other, like you said, and marriage ... my God, Attico. This is the real world."

"So ... you're saying no."

"I'm saying we need to talk about it some more." She gave him a half smile. "I know that's not remotely romantic and God, I wish I were more reckless because then I'd be saying yes, yes, yes ... I do want to spend the rest of my life with you, Attico, I really do." She was silent for a long moment. "If I said yes ...

"Do say yes. Say yes right now." He had a mischievous, hopeful smile on his face which made him look like a teenage boy. Temple chuckled.

"I love you. And how about this ... *yes*. Yes, I will marry you, Attico Fibonacci ... if we talk through some stuff first."

"Stuff?"

Temple nodded. "I want it to be clear that in the event that we, God forbid, split up, I do not want anything from you. Nothing. No money, no property, no trust funds, nothing. Nil, zilch, nada. Okay?"

Attico frowned. "As if I would let that happen."

"Attico." Her voice was firm, and he sighed.

"Fine. We'll get the lawyers to work something out, but just for now ... just in this moment, say yes, Temple."

Temple cupped his face with her palms, her thumbs stroking over his cheeks. "Yes," she said simply. "Yes, Attico, I will marry you."

CHAPTER TWELVE

T emple stood at the window of Attico's Upper East Side apartment and gazed out over Central Park. Three weeks in the States. Three weeks since she'd said yes to Attico's marriage proposal.

Three hours until she would say yes again at the end of an aisle. Attico had kept his promise, and she'd gotten her prenup, guaranteeing her nothing but what she entered the marriage with. He'd argued of course, telling her she should at least have half his earnings for the period they were married—not that he'd ever let her go, of course—but she'd refused and he'd acquiesced reluctantly. "Not that it will ever be an issue," he said with feeling. "This is it. You and Me. We're endgame."

Temple nodded. "We are, my darling love. That I believe with all my heart."

She'd had to compromise, of course. Attico wanted to show her off, show the world how much he loved her, and so, instead of the quiet City Hall wedding she had hoped for, it was to be a high-society wedding.

Tony, Attico's fun older brother, had been a godsend, easing her passage into the family. Sebastiano Fibonacci, she'd quickly realized, was a good man but a drunk. The first time she and Attico had dinner with him, he'd been three sheets before they'd even arrived. When Attico had introduced him, the older man had embraced both of Temple's cheeks, his breath smelling of scotch, and had nodded approvingly at Attico. "She's a beauty, all right. Come on, let's get to know each other."

Sebastiano had been a charmer when he was young, Temple could see that, and he had regaled them with tales of his sons from their childhood. Despite his obvious drinking problem, Temple had liked him very much, but she had noticed that Attico was quieter around his father.

Indeed, he seemed subdued the entire dinner, but later, when she asked him what was wrong, he shrugged. "My dad and my brother have enough energy for us all. It never made sense for me to be as outgoing as them."

She smiled at him. "True colors? My man is a shy boy."

Attico grinned ruefully. "I admit, I am. In truth, it's you who has brought me out of myself. You give me confidence."

Temple was floored by his admission—and a little bemused. "Attico, you're gorgeous, sexy, a successful businessman—and it's *me* who gives *you* confidence?"

"Yup."

Temple shook her head. "I'm honored, but really, what the hell made you *un*confident?"

Attico had smiled but didn't answer her, distracting her with his sweet kisses, but the admission had haunted Temple ever since. What had happened to Attico? She couldn't fathom it.

Attico had wanted to marry her immediately but she'd at least wanted to get acclimated to New York first. Tony had taken over the business while Attico introduced her to the city, first with all the tourist spots she had been excited over—the Empire State Building, the Brooklyn Bridge, Central Park amongst them. She shed a tear at the 9/11 Memorial, laying a flower on the names of some of the victims. In the evenings, they would attend functions at the Met and

MOMA. They took in a ballet, marveling over the performances of the dancers, including Prima Ballerina Boheme Dali.

It was at one of these functions that Temple met Attico's ex-girl-friend, Lucinda. As Attico pointed out the willowy blonde with the perfect little baby bump across the room, Temple felt a jolt. The woman was everything she was not—elegant, graceful, patrician. Temple felt like a fat cousin in comparison. Attico saw her face fall a little and kissed her. "You are more beautiful than Lucinda could ever wish to be, inside and out. Not to say smarter, funnier ... all the '*ers*'."

He grinned at her but still she felt a little inferior when he introduced her.

Lucinda, to her credit, was friendly enough, shaking Temple's hand and complimenting her dark red dress. "Gorgeous color, and the cut is divine."

"It's just an old thing."

Lucinda smiled kindly. "All my favorites are like that. I'm looking forward to getting back into them after this one is born. Nothing like a comfy old favorite and you make that look even better."

Temple smiled at her. "When is he or she due?"

"December, hopefully before Christmas." Lucinda studied her. "You're wondering how I moved on from Attico so quickly?"

"It's none of my business, really."

Lucinda shrugged. "It's okay. I loved Attico, I still do, but it wasn't ... romantic. It was more like best friends for a long time, and I *know* that most relationships end up that way ... but not like us. Attico and me ... we didn't make sense at the end." She looked over to a handsome man with salt-and-pepper hair and a thick, dark beard and smiled fondly. "When I met Pierre, everything was so different, so exciting, and I knew, right then, this was my person."

Temple swallowed, moved by the other woman's honestly. Lucinda smiled at her. "And I think, seeing you two together, that Attico feels that way too. He seems so different, so happy. So fulfilled. I'm glad he has you, Temple."

"Thank you. I mean it."

Lucinda squeezed her arm. "Promise me we can have lunch or just hang out sometimes?"

"I'd like that."

SHE WAS STILL THINKING about what Lucinda said as she excused herself and went to find the ladies' restroom. She didn't know how she would fit into this world, but with people like Lucinda, she knew she would find it a lot easier.

She washed her hands and was leaving the bathrooms when a man bumped into her, apologizing.

"I'm so sorry—well, hello again."

Temple blinked and half-smiled. "Um ..."

The man grinned, offering her his hand. "I'm sorry. We met briefly at Maceo Bartoli's exhibition in Paris. Denny Fleet?"

"Oh, of course, I'm sorry. How are you?"

"Very well, thank you. I assume you're here with Mr. Fibo ... oh." He saw the ring Attico had given her on her ring finger. Denny's smile faltered a little. "Congratulations."

Temple felt uncomfortable. "Thank you. Well, I must get back."

"Of course."

As she walked away, he called to her. "Miss Dubois?"

As Temple turned back to the man, he gave her a chilly smile. "Look after yourself." And he was gone.

Temple sighed. Both times she had met the man, there had been something about him that gave her the yips. She found her way back to Attico's side, finding him talking to Lucinda. They had seemed to be arguing, but both smiled at her when she approached. Lucinda gave her a piece of paper. "My number, Temple. If you need to know where to shop for your wedding dress, or just anything."

"Thank you," Temple said gratefully. "You will come to the wedding? I mean," she looked between them, suddenly nervous. "If it won't be too weird, I mean."

Attico nodded. "Not weird at all. Lu, we'd love you to come."

Lucinda smiled at Temple. "Count me in. Now you *have* to call so we can girl shop together."

"I will, I promise, and thank you again."

Lucinda touched her arm, smiled at Attico and left them. Attico kissed Temple. "You really are the sweetest."

"She's lovely, Atti. I can see why you had a hard time letting her go."

"Meeting you made me see the light, not that I'll ever regret my time with Lu. Hey, shall we skip the rest of the party?" He locked his fingers with hers. "I've had enough champagne. I want a pizza, beer, and a night on the sofa with you."

"Homeboy."

"You know it."

Temple stepped out of her dress and gratefully pulled on her comfy sweater dress. Attico had already changed into his jeans and was wandering around the kitchen shirtless, gathering supplies. The pizza was on its way and Attico grabbed some cold beers from the refrigerator on his way to join her on the sofa.

Temple curled her body into his as he sat down and he looped his arm around her shoulders. "Better?" She was finding it hard to resist kissing his bare chest. God, he smelled good, like warm spice and fresh laundry.

He grinned at her. "Definitely. Will you regret landing yourself with an old man who prefers staying home to parties?"

"Never. And less of the old. There's not that many years between us, Atti. And who cares anyway?" She leaned down and flicked his nipple with her tongue. "How long did the pizza guy say he would be?"

"A half hour."

"Good."

She straddled him, taking his hand and guiding it beneath her dress. Attico's eyes lit up when he encountered bare flesh. "Damn, Temple ..."

She pulled her dress over her head and he smiled. "You're stunning."

Her fingers were at his fly; she could already feel his hard-on through his jeans and when she freed it from his underwear, it sprang up, hard, thick, and long.

Attico dipped his head to suck at her nipples as she plucked a condom from his back pocket and rolled it down his cock. Guiding him inside, she began to ride him.

"Christ, your cunt is so tight and wet, baby," he groaned and buried his face in the valley between her breasts, before returning his mouth to her nipples, biting down gently on each as she urged him to be rough with her.

"Temple ..."

"Take me, Atti, fuck me hard ... leave your mark on my skin."

With a growl he tumbled her to the floor, ramming his hips hard against hers, his mouth rough on hers, kissing her until they both tasted blood. He pinned her hands to the floor, completely masterful, dominating her every move and Temple felt arousal and excitement exploding through her at his touch.

He made her come twice before they had to hurriedly dressed as the pizza delivery guy leaned on the buzzer. Temple got the giggles as she hid her nakedness behind the door, as Attico paid the man, thanking him for the pizza.

She grinned at him as he closed the door. "You are a very naughty girl, Temple Dubois."

She took the pizza box from him and set it down, curling her body around his. "Show me just how naughty, Attico."

The pizza got cold.

CHAPTER THIRTEEN

T emple smiled to herself now as she opened the door of the apartment to the hairdressers and stylists Attico had hired for her. She sighed with relief as she saw Lucinda behind them and hugged her new friend. "Thank God you're here. I have no idea how these things work."

Lucinda laughed. "Well, relax. Honestly, all you have to worry about is being pampered." She ran an eye over the gathered stylists. "Good, they're the best money could get. Atti knows his stuff."

Temple felt out of her depth but Lucinda's presence helped calm her. Over the last couple of weeks, the blonde had gone out of her way to make Temple feel accepted into the Upper East Side social scene and Temple was grateful to the other woman, even if she couldn't quite believe that Lucinda was so accepting of her into Attico's life.

Nevertheless, for now, she would sit back and let the stylists make her over for her wedding. The dress she and Lucinda had chosen was simple, almost Grecian in design. The hairstylists piled her dark hair on top of her head and slid the delicate hair ornament Temple had inherited from her mother into it, affixing the long veil underneath.

Simple, natural makeup and a smiling Lucinda made Temple

look at her reflection in the full-length mirror. Temple could hardly believe it was her. The woman looking back at her was exquisitely beautiful, eyes wide and excited, cheeks flushed with a rosy pink glow.

"That's not me," she said. "You've taped someone else's photo over the mirror."

Lucinda laughed. "Attico told me that you underestimate yourself all the time. Look at you, Temple. You're lovely, just lovely. Now, no tears."

Temple turned to her and hugged her tightly. "You've been so wonderful, Lucinda. I've been waiting for the bubble to burst ever since I've been in New York but it hasn't. Thank you. I don't know how I would have gotten through today without you and I had no right to ask so much of you. You're Attico's ex, for chrissakes."

Lucinda, whose eyes were shining with tears too, laughed. "Maybe because I feel more like his sister than his ex-girlfriend. Both Attico and I are with the right people now. And I'm so happy, so grateful he found you."

Temple bit her lip. "I was going to walk myself down the aisle ... would it be too much to ask you to stand up with me? You can say no, and I won't be offended."

"I would be honored, my friend. Truly."

AND SO, as she walked down the aisle in the ballroom of the hotel, she took Lucinda's arm and the two women moved to where Attico was waiting for Temple, Tony at his side. He grinned at Lucinda, mouthed *'Thank you'* at her, then turned his gaze to Temple. His eyes were intense, full of fire and love, and he bent his head to kiss her cheek. "You're beautiful, just beautiful. I'm the luckiest man in the world."

Temple felt giddy, exhilarated, and before she knew it, they were married and Attico was leading her back down the aisle, through a cloud of flower petals showered by their guests—most of whom Temple didn't know.

The rest of the wedding was a whirl of laughter, greetings, congratulations, and celebration. Even Sebastiano was sober—for most of the day, at least—and the party went on into the night.

AT 3:00 a.m. the guests started to drift away, and Attico and Temple finally got to have a moment to themselves. He spirited her up to their bedroom where she gratefully stripped off her wedding dress. As comfortable as it was, she was relieved to finally change into a simple spaghetti-strap dress.

Attico, too, put on more comfortable clothes, jeans and a vintage T-shirt that brought out the green in his eyes.

Before they went back down to the remainder of their guests, they took a moment, out on the balcony of the hotel. Attico took her in his arms. "Hello, Mrs. Fibonacci."

Temple grinned. "Mr. *Dubois*."

Attico laughed. "I'm not presuming anything. Well, except one thing."

"And what is that?" She laughed at the wicked gleam in his eyes and he pulled her even closer.

"I," he began as his lips found her neck, "am going to fuck you on this balcony later, my darling wife, and fuck you so hard that the whole of Manhattan will hear you scream my name."

Temple reached down and squeezed his groin. "You better keep that promise, husband."

DOWNSTAIRS, they chatted to the remainder of their guests. Temple got to ask who a couple of them were and when she saw a familiar face, she pointed him out to Attico.

Her stomach gave an unpleasant lurch when she saw Attico's smile fade and irritation cross his face. "What is it?"

"I don't believe that guy. He's everywhere."

"Denny Fleet?"

Attico looked at her sharply. "You know him?"

Temple frowned. "I thought you did. He was in Paris. Introduced himself as a business associate."

"Of mine?"

She nodded and Attico snorted. "I know him from the gym, that's all." His brow was furrowed. "He was in Geneva too."

"That's weird."

"It's creepy."

Temple sighed. "It is a little ... but look, let's be positive. Maybe he's just a lonely guy ... with a huge crush on you."

Attico didn't laugh. "We don't need any more weirdness around us." He began to walk over to the man but Fleet saw him, nodded, and turned away, talking to another guest.

"Maybe he's a plus-one."

"Maybe. But I'm going to have someone look into his story."

Temple tugged on his arm. "Not tonight, baby. Tonight is our time, okay?"

Attico relaxed. "Fine." He kissed her, and she leaned into him. "Shall we make our excuses?"

"I think we've done our time."

IN THE ELEVATOR back up to their suite, Attico pressed her up against the wall as he kissed her, moving her arms above her head, pressing his body against hers. "Christ, you're beautiful," he murmured, gazing deep into her eyes.

When he was like this, so intense, so masterful, it took her breath away. Temple kissed him back, grinding her sex against his groin. As the elevator reached their floor, Attico suddenly picked her up and threw her over his shoulder. Temple giggled all the way back to their room.

"Leave the lights off ... we're going to the balcony."

Temple felt her sex flood with excitement at his commanding tone and as he put her down, she leaned back against the stone balcony. Attico dropped to his knees, snaking his hands under her dress and twisting his fingers into the sides of her panties. He drew them down her legs, looking up at her from under his thick, dark lashes, his green eyes bright with desire.

Temple shivered with pleasure at the expression in them. "I love you so much, Attico," she whispered and then gasped as he grinned and buried his face in her sex, his tongue seeking her clit.

"Oh God, Atti ..." She closed her eyes and leaned back, the hard stone cold against her back. Attico's fingers were digging into the soft flesh of her inner thigh as he pleasured her, and neither of them saw the stranger standing in the shadows of the room, observing them.

HE WATCHED THEM MAKE LOVE, his eyes glued to Temple's exquisite body, her plump, full breasts as she pressed them against Attico's chest, her soft belly against her husband's as his cock plowed into her.

His gut twisted with rage and jealousy. He'd let them have their peace and now it was time to put his plan into action. The student in Switzerland had just been his opening salvo.

Now he would make their lives hell.

14

CHAPTER FOURTEEN

The text came through the day after their wedding. Attico, having neglected his work, had agreed with Tony that he would go into the office for a day before he and Temple left for their honeymoon.

Temple was alone when the message came through. She was packing their cases for their trip—a week in Antigua—and wasn't thinking when she opened the message.

The Devil tarot card flashed up on her screen and she winced and dropped the phone. Trembling, she picked it up, trying to see if there was a further message, but there was none. She sat down on the floor, studying the iconography, trying to decipher the message.

The Devil was depicted as a vengeful god, standing over the body of a dead woman, laughing. The woman stared sightlessly to the skies, her robes soaked with blood, run through with swords. The Devil bore the last one, raising above his head, ready to deliver the coup de grâce to the stricken woman.

Temple was trembling. Olivia's death had followed the last time she had received this kind of message but the school was closed. Was it a threat to her own life, this time? And why, for the love of God? And if someone meant to kill her, why would he or she warn her first?

The killer must know that she was protected by Attico's wealth and power.

She called Attico and told him. "I'm coming home," he said immediately.

"No, no, don't. I'm fine and it's not like this place isn't a fortress, anyway. I don't want to be one of those hysterical wives, I just needed to hear your voice."

"I don't like this, Tem. Someone's fucking around with you and— wait, excuse me, honey ..." Temple heard someone else in the room talking, then Attico spoke her name.

"I'm here."

"Baby, something's happened ... Stay where you are and my security team is on its way. Please, sweetheart, do everything they ask of you."

"What's going on, Atti?"

He hesitated. "Darling ... I'll be home as fast as I can and then I'll tell you everything. Please, just stay there."

TEMPLE PACED THE ROOM, shooting worried glances at the two hulking bodyguards who had appeared moments after Attico's call. They stood like statues, but their eyes flicked around the room, watching her every move. When she went to open the window, one of them stopped her. "Please, Mrs. Fibonacci, stay away from the windows."

God. Anxiety made her stomach clench. Was this normal in Attico's world? She grabbed her cell phone. She would call Lucinda, ask her if this happened when she was with Atti—she started as the same bodyguard put a gentle hand on her arm. "I'm sorry, ma'am. Mr. Fibonacci said no phone calls in or out. Just until he returns."

Holy hell. Temple gave a tight nod then sat down, clasping her trembling hands together. It felt like an age before Attico returned, his face set and grim. He nodded at the guards who left them alone then came to her. "I'm sorry, darling, I didn't want to scare you."

"What's going on?"

Attico made her sit down, and Temple was horrified to find that his eyes were red, his distress evident. "Sweetheart ... I have some distressing news. God, I can't even believe I'm going to say these words. It's Lu."

The anxiety was turning to horror. Temple swallowed hard. "Attico ..."

"She was walking to the subway, and someone stabbed her in the back and pushed her down the staircase."

Temple's hand was at her mouth. "Oh God, no ..."

"She's in the hospital. The baby ... he didn't make it. The stab wound wasn't so deep but Lu hit her head pretty badly. They've been operating since she got to the hospital. Pierre is with her."

"Oh no, no ... poor Lucinda. Who the hell would want to hurt her?"

"That's just it." He sighed and passed a hand over his eyes. He looked exhausted. "Before she was pushed, her attacker said something loud enough to be heard by witnesses. He said 'You can blame Fibonacci and his ...' I'm sorry, darling, I'm just repeating what he said. 'You can blame Fibonacci and his ... whore for this.'"

Temple got up and ran to the bathroom where she threw up and up. Attico followed her, rubbing her back, holding her hair back for her as she vomited. "I debated whether to tell you any of this."

Temple shook her head. "Attico, no. Never keep anything like this from me ... and God, do you think he's picking off everyone we love? The card I got today, the picture on the text message ... it was The Devil."

She rinsed out her mouth and went to get her cell phone. She showed Attico the card. Now that they studied it, she saw that the dead woman was pregnant. *Oh God ...*

Attico sighed, shaking his head. "I don't think there's any doubt now. Your brother, Olivia, and now Lu. Someone's playing dangerous games."

THE POLICE CAME to see them, the detectives polite as Attico and Temple told them everything they knew. One of the detectives,

Halloran nodded. "The FBI will want to know about this. They'll be in touch with the Geneva authorities." She looked at Temple. "I'm sorry for your loss, Mrs. Fibonacci."

"Thank you." Temple's throat felt thick.

"I'm taking my wife out of the country for a week," Attico told them, to Temple's dismay.

"Darling, what about Lu?"

"It's my understanding that Mr. Pierre Latulip has asked that Lucinda have no visitors except immediate family?" Halloran again and Attico nodded, his eyes sad.

"That's right."

"Then I think it's a good idea for you and Mr. Fibonacci to get away. You'll be taking protection, of course?"

Attico nodded and he and the detectives talked some more. Temple felt empty. Poor Lucinda ... her heart ached for her friend and her loss. Temple couldn't imagine. And it was clear now that she and Attico were the reason. No wonder Pierre didn't want them at the hospital. God, what a fucking mess.

It wasn't until after the police officers left that she realized something. "How the hell did he get my new number?"

"Who have you given it out to?"

"Hardly anyone. You, obviously, Dean Corke, Zella, Lucinda. Some of the wedding planners and stylists. Nicolai."

She gave a half smile now. Nicolai. Her best friend and she'd hardly spoken to him since graduation. He hadn't been able to make it to their wedding, much to her sadness, but he had a commitment he couldn't break.

"I'll be with you in spirit, *ma petite pamplemousse*," he'd said when she had spoken to him over the phone. He made her laugh, and she missed having him around.

Attico cupped her cheek in his palm. "Are you okay?"

"No. But I will be." She slid her arms around his waist. "I just need to know that everyone I love is safe. Especially you. If anything ever happened to you, Attico ... I couldn't go on. I mean it."

He pressed his lips to her forehead. "Don't say things like that, baby."

"It's true."

Attico sighed. "For me too."

They stood just holding each other for a time, then Attico smoothed her hair away from her face. "Let's pack. If I'm to take you away, then we might as well have our ..."

"Don't. I mean, I'll go away with you but let's not call this our honeymoon. Not while Lu is still in danger and that madman is out there."

"Okay, baby."

WHILE THEY WERE PACKING, Temple grabbed her cell phone and send Lucinda a message.

DARLING LU, I'm so sorry. If there's anything I can do ... anything. Love to you and Pierre. I mean it.

Anything.

Temple.

SHE FELT LIKE CRYING, with sadness, yes, but even more with anger. Who was this bastard and why the hell was he targeting them? In her heart, she knew the person who had killed Luc and Olivia was the same one who had tried to murder Lucinda.

"Baby, at our wedding you said you would ask a detective to look into Denny Fleet. Did you ever?"

Attico stopped what he was doing. "No. I admit it slipped my mind. Wait, I'll call Tony and asked him to get one of our regular guys on it."

BY THE TIME they were taking off from Teterboro in Attico's jet, Tony had promised them that he would look into Denny Fleet's background.

"It seems odd that he would be everywhere you've been over the last few months, Atti. Don't worry, I'm on it."

Temple was in the bedroom when Attico finished chatting to the pilot and he laid down beside her. "I called the hospital. Lu's out of surgery and they said it went well."

"They told you that? When you're not a relative?"

Attico gave a sheepish smile. "I have my ways."

"The awesome power of money." Temple didn't mean the edge to creep into her voice but right now she was pissed at the world.

Attico shrugged off her jibe. "It is what it is."

Temple closed her eyes and Attico pulled her close. "I swear, Tem, we'll beat this. You and me, remember? Nothing's going change that."

"I know. Just ... promise me you'll always tell me the truth about everything. Don't protect me by either withholding or lying. That's the one thing I can't cope with."

"I promise, baby."

BUT WHEN TEMPLE FELL ASLEEP, exhausted from shock and grief, Attico found he could not sleep. *Don't withhold anything from me ...*

Attico grimaced. If Temple knew what he hadn't told her from the start ... what the hell would she do?

She would leave you in an instant and you would deserve it.

Jesus, no. He couldn't bear to imagine his life without her now. It would be intolerable and yet, by continuing to keep what he knew about the Winter Blood Tarot, about Luc, about what he had done ... he had already begun to regret not telling her up front.

Damn stupid decision made by a selfish man.

If anything happened to anyone else, or to Temple—God, the thought made pain shoot straight through him—then Attico would go mad, he knew it.

Whoever it was threatening his love, his friends, he would make them pay.

Whatever the cost.

CHAPTER FIFTEEN

B y the third day of their *not*-honeymoon, Temple and Attico had relaxed enough to begin to enjoy their time on the tropical island, although every day Attico would get calls from Tony updating him.

Temple felt drained. She knew from Attico's contacts at the hospital that Lucinda was doing much better. The stab wound she had received had been little more than a flesh wound, and her head injuries were not as serious as first thought.

But there was still the tragedy of the lost baby and Temple couldn't help but feel guilty. As Attico spoke to Tony on the Thursday afternoon, she went to sit on the private beach outside of the villa Attico had rented for them. It was hot, but Temple couldn't feel anything but cold inside. Luc was dead. Olivia was dead. Lucinda's baby ...

The worst thing was, apart from the grief and the guilt, that she was looking at everyone she had ever met, spoken to, looked at, passed on the street and wondering if it was them who was making them all suffer, causing so much pain.

Even Attico. None of this had happened until they met. Was it some weird kind of cosmic balance that as happy as she was with him, there had to be some kind of ... payback?

And even worse ... she knew he was keeping something from her about his time at the Academy and his knowledge of Luc. Had Attico known the girl who died? She tried to remember his reaction when she'd taken him to see the Winter Blood Tarot. He'd seemed not to recognize it, but was he just a good actor?

She wondered if Dean Corke knew more about Attico than he'd told her. She would try to call him when they got back to New York, depending on whether Attico let her call *anyone*. He was a fair, good man, but now she could see—he was used to being in charge.

Temple brought herself up sharply. *What the hell are you thinking? Attico would never stop me from doing anything.* She looked over her shoulder, through the French windows at the man she had married.

The man she had married after only a few weeks. What had she been thinking? Think logically.

One. You love him.

Yes, but do I really know him?

What does that have to do with love? Plenty of people fall in love with someone they don't know.

"Ahh." Temple groaned at herself. The only thing she knew for sure right now was that yes, she did love Attico Fibonacci. She got up, dusted the sand off her dress, and went inside.

Attico was still talking to someone on the telephone and so Temple busied herself tidying up the kitchen. The villa was beautiful, an absolute haven away from the horrors they had been experiencing, but Temple couldn't settle. She felt guilty for running away from their problems.

Slowly, Attico's conversation began to creep into her consciousness. She looked over to him and he smiled back at her, blowing her a kiss. She smiled but couldn't help wonder who he was talking to now. His tone was softer than when he was talking to Tony and now, when he ended the call, he was smiling.

"That was Lu. They've released her from hospital. Obviously, she and Pierre are having to come to terms with the loss of their child, but physically, she's doing much better." He got up and went to Temple, stroking his hand through her hair, looping it back over her ear. "She sends her love, Tem."

Temple let out a shaky breath. "She's okay?"

Attico nodded. "As well as can be expected."

Temple felt her body slump, a release of tension. Attico drew her into his arms and she closed her eyes. "Baby, come lay down with me."

He led her into the bedroom and they lay on the bed together, Attico's hand stroking down her body. Temple felt a myriad of emotions going through her, but for now, she just wanted one.

Love.

She pressed her lips to her husband's, feeling him respond, his kiss becoming deep, his tongue caressing hers. Attico gave a soft groan as he covered her body with his, pushing up her dress over her hips.

"Don't wait," Temple said urgently, "I need you inside me."

With one swift movement, Attico ripped her panties from her as she freed his cock from his underwear and then he was inside her, thrusting hard, his hands pinning hers to the bed. Their lovemaking was fierce, animal, almost desperate as they coupled furiously, the bed moving with their exertions.

Temple came hard, crying out his name again and again, then as they recovered, she pushed him onto his back and straddled him. Attico grinned up at her. "Do you like that dress?"

Temple shrugged. "It's okay. Why?"

Attico grabbed the fabric on her shoulder and tore it from her. Temple grinned. "Bad boy."

"I'm going to rip this whole thing from your delicious body and then I'm going to have you in every way you can imagine."

Temple almost purred with arousal as Attico ripped the rest of the dress from her body, tumbling her back onto the bed and trailing his lips down the length of her belly. He pushed her legs up to her chest, pushing her thighs apart. "Christ, that's the most exquisite view on this earth ..."

Temple felt her sex flood with desire as Attico's cock plunged back into her and he fucked her hard, her thighs screaming with sweet pain as he rammed his hips against hers, his cock driving deeper and harder into her cunt.

"God, Attico, Attico ..."

She came again, feeling almost unhinged, a million stars exploding in her head as her orgasm ripped through her. Attico reached his climax, and she felt him pump thick, creamy cum deep inside her. As they caught their breath, Temple reveled in the feel of his seed inside her. She'd been on birth control since before the wedding, but she loved the feeling of his skin on hers. It made her feel closer to him.

Attico smiled over at her. "I hope you're not tired because that was just the start of a very long night."

Temple laughed, a blessed release of tension and they began again and Temple felt happiness seep into her bones.

BUT THE NEXT MORNING, the third card was sent to her and it changed everything.

CHAPTER SIXTEEN

he Lovers. The most romantic card in the Tarot deck ... *usually*.

But the Lovers card in the Winter Tarot was the opposite of romantic. Yes, the two lovers depicted were entwined together, kissing, but at the same time, the man's hand was on the hilt of a knife, the blade of which was buried deep inside the woman's body. Blood streaked down what looked like a wedding dress, and her head fell backwards, hair streaming down her back as she died.

And this time the text message came with a warning.

How well do you really know your husband?

Temple cursed softly and turned her phone off. Something was telling her not to tell Attico about it, despite the threat, but she didn't know what. Trust. Did she trust Attico as well as love him?

She kept the message a secret as they flew back to New York, deciding to tell him when she thought it was the right time. For now ...

"Babe? Tony's detective came through with some stuff about Denny Fleet."

She looked up as Attico came back into their kitchen. "Oh?"

His face was grim, though. "Yep. He came up with the fact that Denny Fleet … doesn't exist."

Temple put down her cup of coffee. "What?"

"Doesn't exist. There is no Denny Fleet, it's a pseudonym." Attico sighed and sat down. "He—whoever he is—has been watching us, following us. And I have no idea why."

"He was in Geneva when Luc died, when Olivia was murdered. It has to be connected, right?"

"I think so too."

Temple sighed. "Maybe he was a relative of the girl who was killed back then. He wants revenge … except …"

"Except?"

She shook her head. "Why wait until now? Luc was in the facility for twenty years, unprotected."

Attico studied her. "You're sure of Luc's guilt?"

"I used to think so … but what if it was an accident, a game gone wrong? There was a society … did you know about it? Based around the Winter Blood Tarot?"

Attico hesitated a beat before answering. "No."

Temple felt a shock go through her. *He's lying* … She looked away from his gaze. "Well, there was. Dean Corke hasn't told me a great deal about it, but what he did tell me was that it began as a theatrical society. That they wrote scripts based on each of the Major Arcana in the pack and intended to perform them but then they found the girl stabbed to death."

She got up and moved around the room, not wanting him to touch her. *Liar … Liar … No, give him a chance.*

"Luc was part of the society, the only one the police ever questioned. Everyone else was too … rich to be a suspect. They didn't find any proof but by then Luc was desperate. His friends turned away from him."

She met Attico's gaze then. "And you weren't part of the society?"

"No. I swear I wasn't. I had no idea it existed."

Temple turned away from him. "That might be a reason Fleet

came after me, after the people I love. Revenge. I just don't know, otherwise, unless ..."

"Unless?"

"Unless I'm not the target. Unless it's someone else. Like you, Attico."

He went very still. "What are you saying, Temple?"

Oh God. Here it comes. She squared up to him. "You're lying to me, Attico. You have been lying to me from the start. You knew Luc. You knew about the society."

"No ..." Attico stopped, sat down, and dropped his face into his hands. "Okay. All right. Yes, I knew about the society. But Temple, I swear to God, I had nothing to do with it. I just ... it was Tony. My brother. Although he had graduated more than a decade earlier, he was still heavily involved with the school. When the girl died, I could tell he was absolutely devastated. Turned out ... she had been his lover. When she died, she was pregnant with his child. They never questioned him because my father stepped in."

"Money buying innocence." Temple made a disgusted noise.

Attico's face hardened. "Maybe. But Tony is no more a murderer than I am."

"And neither was Luc."

"Are you absolutely sure?"

Temple whirled around, furious now. "Are you? Luc had no reason to kill anyone. I'm assuming, since you're so sure, that Tony had no reason either? Despite the fact he'd gotten a poor girl pregnant? Must have been quite the embarrassment for your family. But then again, you Fibonaccis are good at seducing the paupers of the parish, aren't you?"

Attico was angry now. "What the fuck are you talking about? Are you having some sort of pity party over there, Temple? Haven't I always maintained that money had nothing to do with how I feel about you?"

Temple stalked out of the room but Attico wasn't about to let her get away. "Don't turn away from me, Tem. We have to talk about this."

Temple grabbed her phone and shoved it at him. "Look at the last text message."

Attico flicked to the image of the card and read the message beneath. The fight seemed to go out of him. He looked up at Temple, his eyes haunted. "Temple ... I would never hurt you. You know that."

Temple stepped close to him. "I know that. Not physically. But my question is what would you do to protect me? Or anyone you love?"

Attico looked aghast. "You think I could hurt someone?"

"Yes."

Attico looked staggered. "Wow. Oh wow."

Temple felt a little guilty. This fight had gotten way out of hand. "What I mean is ..."

"I know what you mean." He looked sick. He sat on the edge of the bed.

"Just if you saw someone hurting me or Tony or your dad ..." Temple's fury was abating now. How the hell had they gotten to the point where she'd accused him of ... what?

Murder?

No. She sat down next to him. "I'm sorry, I lost my temper."

"But you must have been thinking those things," he said softly and looked at her with pain-filled eyes. "I guess we don't know each other that well."

"I guess not." Her heart thumped sadly. "Did we make a mistake?"

"I don't want to believe we did ..."

"... but ..."

"But," he agreed, nodding.

Temple sighed, tears close to the surface now. "Maybe we should take some time apart."

He leaned his forehead against hers. "I don't want to lose you."

"Me either. But we did go into this too fast and at a time of heightened emotion."

He smoothed her hair away from her face. "It won't change the way I feel about you."

"We need to do this." It was breaking her heart to say the words, but she knew in her gut it was the right thing to do. "I'll go back to Geneva for a while."

"No, please." Tears were streaming down his handsome face and Temple burst into tears, but although he tried to dissuade her all night long, pleading with her to stay, she wouldn't be moved.

ATTICO INSISTED on her taking the Fibonacci jet back to Geneva. "For your security, for my peace of mind. Please."

Her heart was breaking at the thought of leaving him but they needed some space so she agreed. At the airport, he touched the ring on her finger. "Please remember this. Remember me. Remember I love you with all my heart, that you are my person. For all time, Temple."

She was still crying when the plane took off.

BACK IN GENEVA, she was astonished but grateful when she saw Nicolai waiting for her. "How did you know?"

"Attico called me," Nicolai admitted, hugging her tightly. "What's going on, Temple?"

Attico, not wanting her to be unsafe alone in the city, had arranged a new apartment for her, despite her insistence that she could find her own, but eventually she acquiesced to his wishes.

She and Nicolai went back to it now, finding it already furnished and with a fridge full of food and alcohol. "Hey, I might swap Rainer for your hubby," Nicolai said cheerfully. "Well, if you don't want him anymore."

Temple knew he was kidding, but she winced painfully and he saw. "Sorry, Tem, a bad joke. Look, let's grab some beer and you can tell me what the hell is going on with you."

TEMPLE TOLD HIM EVERYTHING, and even to her own ears, none of it made sense. "So let me get this right. You meet Attico, then all this crap starts. Bear in mind, it also coincided with the arrival of the Winter Blood Tarot, the history of which is pretty dark. Then Luc is killed, Olivia, and your friend in New York is hurt. You marry a guy you've known only for a few weeks, and now you've left him."

"I haven't left him; we're just taking some space."

"None of this makes sense, Temple."

She sighed. "I know. I just have to sort my head out. I think maybe I need to grieve Luc and Olivia, maybe talk to the dean and the police here again. They haven't contacted me for weeks about Luc's death now and I think they've given up trying to find whoever killed him."

"And this Fleet guy?"

"That's what I want to ask the dean. We know so little about the original murder victim."

Nicolai grinned at her. "So you're here doing detective work?"

"I just think this whole situation is crazy and I need to know more about who would want to kill Luc. It has to be tied into the tarot and the old murder, right?"

Nicolai sighed. "I don't know, honey. All I know is that someone is messing with you, messing with your head, your life, your marriage. I'm not sure coming back to Geneva was the safest thing for you to do."

NEITHER OF THEM knew just how horrifically his words were about to come true.

CHAPTER SEVENTEEN

F orty-eight hours without Temple and Attico felt like he was
going crazy. He called her multiple times a day, was grateful
when she took each call, only a little remonstrative about his
endless worry. "I'm fine, baby, I promise. There's always someone
around me."

"I wish you would let me send a security team."

"No, thank you. I hate being caged."

But he had a team over there anyway, out of Temple's sight. They
were ordered to keep a distance unless she was in trouble. He would
deal with her anger when and if he needed to.

On a Monday, a week after Temple had left, Attico couldn't
concentrate at work and decided to drive out to his father's place.
Sebastiano had been unnaturally quiet of late and Attico wondered if
he was mired in his drinking as happened periodically before Sebastiano went on a tear and decided to kick the habit.

To his welcome surprise, Sebastiano appeared not only sober but
active. A spritely seventy-year-old, with the same bright green eyes as
his son, clapped his son on the back. "And where's the lovely
Temple?"

Attico hadn't told his father about the temporary separation and now he fudged it again. "She's just gone back to Geneva for a while to prepare for the new school year."

"I see. Want a drink?" Sebastiano smiled at his son's raised eyebrows. "I mean non-alcoholic. I'm juicing. Come with me."

Amused, Attico followed his father to the large kitchen where he saw an array of fruits and vegetables as well as a state-of-the-art juicer on the counter. He grinned. "Wow, Dad, you're really into this."

"Don't mock," Sebastiano said, waving a fruit knife in the air. He began to chop some fruit. "I needed something to distract me from real drink. Here it is, and I have to say, I feel a whole lot better."

"That's great, Dad, really." Attico sat at the counter while his father prepared their drinks.

Sebastiano studied his son. "So, Temple is in Europe?"

Attico nodded and Sebastiano harrumphed. "You're not letting that lovely girl get away now, are you?"

"I won't."

"Won't. Hmm. Tony says there's trouble in paradise."

Attico was annoyed. "He does, does he?"

"He's worried. Look, I don't know Temple as well as you ... *if* you do know her, but I hear that she's Luc Monfils' younger sister. Playing with fire there, Attico."

Attico nodded. "I know."

"That dumb society. Those tarot cards should have been burned when they were found,"

Attico studied his father. "Dad ... have you ever seen the tarot cards?"

Sebastiano nodded. "I have. Utter depravity, if you ask me. I don't give a crap if they're art or not. Sick."

"I agree." Attico fiddled with a piece of kiwi fruit. "Since they've been back at the Academy, all this crap has been dredged up. Now Luc's dead, a girl's been killed, and Temple's being stalked. Not to mention poor Lu."

Sebastiano looked at his son appalled. "And you let Temple go back there alone?"

"Of course not. She didn't want me there but, believe me Dad, there's a team of people looking out after her. She just doesn't know it. They've been ordered to keep their distance unless she needs them, and the apartment I rented for her is state of the art when it comes to security."

Sebastiano nodded, giving his son a half smile. "So, another thing you've kept from her."

Attico sighed. "Dad ..."

"The prenup, that's what I'm talking about."

"Dad, I never intend for us to divorce, but if we do, I'm damn well going to make sure Temple never has to want for anything, ever."

"Against her wishes."

"I'm not apologizing for wanting to make sure she has everything she deserves."

Sebastiano chuckled. "Headstrong. Just like your mother."

Attico shrugged. "Temple will thank me later. Besides, it's not ever going to be an issue; Temple and I are not splitting up."

TEMPLE WALKED through the halls of the Academy, listening to her footsteps ringing in the silence. It seemed odd without the students here—usually summers were full of a new influx of rich kids, eager to study and improve their chances of getting into a good college.

Temple walked to Dean Corke's office. The dean lived at the Academy full-time, had done since his teaching days, and he smiled at her now as she knocked and entered his office.

"Temple, dear, lovely to see you. Have a seat."

She smiled at the elderly man. "Thanks for seeing me, Dean. I know it's your personal time."

Dean Corke sighed. "In other circumstances, Temple, I'd relish the vacation but not this time. Even with the murder twenty years ago, we've never experienced this horror. That girl wasn't a student here—not that it makes it any less tragic—but Olivia Dolenz's death ... I've had parents call and remove their kids from the school. Some you might know. Rosario, Barry Helm."

Temple was dismayed. "God, Dean ... We need to get to the

bottom of this all. That's why I came back, really. I went to see Chief Renard yesterday, but he said they have no leads on either Luc or Olivia or the theft of the tarot." She looked at him steadily. "Dean, I need you to tell me everything you know about what happened back then. Whether or not Attico or Tony Fibonacci had anything to do with the murder ... whether Luc was guilty. Whatever it is, please. Tell me."

Corke looked at her unhappily. "Temple, my dear ... the whole thing was extremely distressing and I ..."

"Dean Corke, someone has been sending me messages, each one a card from the Winter Blood deck. Threatening messages. The last one I received ..." She swallowed hard, remembering the horrific Lovers card. "Well, let's just say it was too close to home."

Attico might not have murdered her as depicted in the card's image, but without him, her heart was breaking. She would rather die than be without him. Temple pushed the thought aside.

Dean Corke sighed. "What do you know?"

She told him she knew that the Winter Blood society had begun as a theater group. He nodded. "Tony Fibonacci was the founder, I know that much. He was working in Geneva then, very involved with the school still. The Fibonaccis have been very generous to us over the years, including now. I received this letter from your husband, pledging a considerable amount to us every year. It may just save the school."

Temple drew in a deep breath. She hated to think like this, but it was just like Attico to make his presence known to her, even now. *I'm here, I have the money, I'm always around.*

God, what was wrong with her? This whole business was making her paranoid, and she was taking it out on the one person she loved with all her heart. "What else, Dean?"

"The group began to put on the plays, to much outcry, of course, but also much acclaim. More students joined, but soon a few of the female attendees began to make complaints about the behavior of some of the boys. At first, they said it was just that the boys seemed to be too committed to their roles, which were invariably that of aggressors. Claims of misogyny, which isn't surprising given the nature of the tarot deck. Some parents objected to the occult nature of the cards and the plays."

Dean Corke rubbed his forehead, looking tired. "Then, after a few years, the group began to dwindle until there were only a few core people left. Luc, Simon LeFevre, Aloysius Harper."

"Attico?"

Dean Corke shook his head. "As far as I know, Attico was never a member of Winter Blood, at least, not openly. Tony tried to persuade him to join, to rally the troops, and I know Attico was close to Luc for a time ..."

"What?" Temple was shocked. "Attico and Luc were friends?"

"Very much so. That's why ... well, perhaps it would be better for you not to know."

Temple's heart was beating against her ribs. "No, tell me. Whatever it is. Tell me."

Corke pondered. "When the girl was found dead ... it was Attico who told the police it was Luc who killed her."

It was like a punch to the gut and Temple bent double, trying to drag air into the lungs that seemed to be frozen in her chest. No. Attico had been the one to accuse Luc? "It can't be."

"I'm so sorry, Temple dear, but it's true. When Luc discovered his friend's betrayal, that's when he leaped from the turrets of this building." The old man looked at her with sympathy. "Attico was heartbroken. He was never the same afterward."

Temple staggered to her feet. "Thank you, Dean." She managed to choke out the words but she knew she had to get out of there. The horror of what she had been told was all-consuming. She heard the dean call her name as she staggered out into the hallways but she ignored him and kept running.

As she ran out into the courtyard, not feeling the hammering rain on her skin, her phone beeped. Another card.

The High Priestess. A woman, bound to a stake, blindfold, a knife thrust deep into her body. Her head hung down, blood streaked down her dress. Temple gasped, knowing this must be the card that had preceded the girl's murder twenty years previously.

The threat was clear. Temple turned, in a blind panic now as she heard a step behind her, but then she was grabbed and her head smashed against the wall of the school and she knew nothing more.

ATTICO WAS PRETENDING to concentrate on work when the call came through from his security team in Geneva. The worst news. The news he had somehow, however dreadful, been expecting.

Temple had been taken. Temple was gone.

CHAPTER EIGHTEEN

T he flight from New York to Geneva seemed to take twice as long as normal. Chief Renard met Attico at the airport and took him straight to the school.

"Dean Corke is very distressed as you can imagine. He had just been talking to Temple when she was taken."

"What had they been talking about?"

Chief Renard didn't answer and Attico sighed. Temple had been doing some digging. He rubbed his head. She had been gone for less than twenty-four hours but Attico knew wherever she was, she was going through hell.

If she was still alive. Attico tried to reason with himself—surely he would know, in his heart, if Temple was already dead. But no, there was none of that hokey gut instinct. He simply didn't know.

They'd found her phone, still open on the message, and when Renard showed him the card she'd been sent, Attico's blood had turned to ice. "Jesus. They're going to kill her."

Renard studied him. "Who? Who are 'they,' Attico?"

Attico shook his head. "I wish I knew."

. . .

TONY HAD FLOWN over with Attico, and now the brothers waited to be questioned by Renard. Tony put his arm around his brother's shoulders but didn't offer any empty words of comfort and Attico was grateful. He didn't want hope now; he just wanted Temple back, safe and in his arms.

Renard called them in. "We may have something. Brett Forrester has disappeared off the face of the map."

"He tried to rape Temple before. He got violent. You think he's behind this?"

"You tell me." Renard looked at Tony. "I believe you were a contemporary of his?"

Tony nodded. "Slime ball. I could well believe he would abduct Temple and try to scare her, but murder? I'm not sure."

"Hmm. Well, he certainly would have had access to the school, the exhibition. Apparently after Temple reported the rape to the Dean, Forrester was fired, but they never revoked his access."

Tony made a disgusted noise, but Attico kept his eyes on the detective. "So, Forrester is the suspect ... what now?"

"We have the airports and borders alerted but, to be honest, if the abductor's intent is, I'm sorry to say, to kill Mademoiselle Dubois ..."

"... Madame Fibonacci," Attico corrected quietly, his voice full of heartbreak. "She's my wife now."

"Forgive me. Of course. Madame Fibonacci." Renard looked at Attico and Attico saw sympathy in his eyes. *He thinks she's already dead. Oh God, please no ...*

"Monsieur Renard ... what can we do? We have unlimited resources to help you. Please, let us help."

"Can I be frank?"

"Of course."

Renard cleared his throat. "I can't decide whether this is about you, the Fibonaccis or about Temple. In one way, it could be revenge for Luc Monfils' actions twenty years ago."

"The victim? She was never identified, is that right?"

Renard hesitated. "Not exactly."

Attico and Tony looked at each other. "What?"

"Her family wanted it hushed up."

"They wanted her murder hushed up?" Attico's voice was full of incredulity.

Renard nodded. "Yes. For what reason ... I simply do not know." He looked at Attico. "They wanted charges pressed against Luc Monfils, obviously, but his accident put paid to that. After that, they simply didn't want their daughter's name dragged through the press."

"Surely that's illegal?"

Renard's lips twitched. "They too had unlimited resources, Mr. Fibonacci."

"Look, this isn't helping Temple." Attico got up and paced the room. "So what? Are we saying it could be the dead girl's relative? What?"

"I told you. We just don't know. All we can do follow the few leads we have. We'll need you to stay and help us out with some questions."

"No problem." Tony glanced at his brother, who nodded stiffly. Attico looked at Renard.

"Just find her. Please."

TEMPLE OPENED her eyes to blackness. She felt the rough material of the blindfold against her lashes, the harsh rub of the rope around her hands. "Hello?" Her voice was gravelly, gruff.

She was lying on her side on a rough blanket, that much she could make out. She was indoors, in a room that smelled of damp and disuse. "Hello?"

No answer and for a moment, she thought she was alone. Then she started, gasped as someone touched her face. "Shh."

A man's voice. She felt him draw a fingertip down her cheek, almost tenderly. "Who are you? What do you want?"

There was something cold against the skin of her arm, then a sharp pinprick and her head whirled. Whatever he'd given her made her feel euphoric at first, then, as the effects faded, her mouth went dry, her skin itched, and she lost any sense of time passing. Eventually, her breathing slowed, and she passed out.

Her unconsciousness was tormented by dreams, blood, death, and worst of all, Attico, losing him, or him turning away from her as she was being killed.

She woke shivering and crying. This time she could sense she was alone and sobbed quietly until she was exhausted. Temple tried to pull her hands free—her shoulders were burning—but whoever had tied her knew what they were doing.

Exhausted, she let her body slump and conjured up a happy memory. The night before her wedding to Attico. She had made him promise to leave by midnight, but that hadn't stopped them from making the most of the few hours left of their last day as single people.

Dinner at one of Attico's favorite restaurants, followed by a taxi ride back to her hotel, where they kissed the entire journey and barely saw any of New York's bustling nightlife outside the cab window. Sharing an elevator with some other guests, they'd held hands and gazed at each other.

In the suite, they'd shared a bottle of champagne on the balcony, Attico's arm around her waist, his lips against her hair. Temple smiled up at him. "I love you, Atti."

Attico smiled down at her, his beautiful green eyes crinkled at the edges, softening the thick brows that often made him look so brooding and dangerous. "As I love you, piccolo."

He bent his head and pressed his lips to hers. As the kiss deepened, he took the champagne flute from her hand and set it down on the balcony, sweeping her up into his arms.

"Where shall we fuck first, little one?"

Temple giggled. "Wherever you want to, baby."

They didn't make it to the bed, instead wrestling each other playfully to the rug and tugging off each other's clothes. Temple ran her hands over his hard chest then linked her arms around his neck. "I'm so lucky," she whispered, "lucky to have found you, lucky to have had you as my first. You've spoiled me for other men—not that I'll ever want anyone else."

"Temple," he murmured, his lips against hers. "My life began when I met you."

His kiss was rough, feral, and Temple sank into it, giving up all her control as Attico dominated her body like only he could.

As he pinned her hands to the floor, she gazed up at him as he smiled down at her. "Wrap your legs around me, beautiful."

She did as he asked and then sighed with pleasure as he slowly entered her. They still used condoms most of the time but now that Temple was on birth control, there were times when they wanted to be skin on skin. His cock, so long, thick, and heavy, filled her and they began to move, completely in sync, utterly uninhibited.

Their lovemaking, as always, began with laughter and fun, but then things became intense, they locked eyes and began to fuck hard, wild, animal-like.

Temple came hard, then squealed as Attico bit down on her sensitive nipples in turn, before he too neared his peak. "Come on my skin," Temple urged. "I want you on my skin."

Attico, his beautiful face flushed red, his eyes shining, withdrew and ejaculated on her belly, groaning her name as she urged him on. He collapsed beside her, panting for air. "Christ, Temple, you drive me crazy ... so crazy ..."

Temple smiled. "I'm glad, baby."

Attico slipped his hand between her legs and massaged her already sensitive clit, stroking her into a mellow orgasm. She cupped his balls in her hand, stroking her thumb over them until his cock was beginning to stiffen again. She smiled up at him. "Atti?"

"Yes, beautiful?"

"Can we try ... I mean, I've been thinking about different, um ..." She felt her face flush hot. "Things. *Sex* ... things."

Attico grinned, and she scowled at him. "Don't make fun, I'm still new to this."

"Sorry. Baby, we can try anything you want as long as you're ready for it. What did you have in mind?"

To answer him, she smiled shy and rolled onto her stomach, opening her legs a little. Attico grinned. "My pleasure, little one."

He moved on top of her, pressing his lips to the back of her neck then trailing them down her spine. Temple shivered with pleasure as he kissed the small of her back. "Just relax, baby," he said, as he pushed her legs apart further and eased gently into her ass. Temple gasped at the sharp pain, then as he began to move, she relaxed into it. He made her come, sighing and moaning, then gently rolled her onto her back. "Okay?"

"More than okay." Temple caught her breath. "I never thought I would do anything like that. I know I must seem so sheltered to you."

"It is surprising to me that you were a virgin, I have to say. Look at you ... you're breathtaking."

She grinned, embarrassed at the compliment, but shook her head. "That doesn't really have to do with it, though, does it? The truth is, it was the last thing left that I had control over. My family was gone, I was beholden to the Academy for my food, my lodgings, my studies, even my career. Nothing was up to me. Only this year did I finally afford my own apartment, Atti."

Attico nodded, his eyes serious. "I get it."

"So, keeping my virginity, however an old-fashioned concept it is, was my little way of saying I belong to *me*. I choose. And I chose you, Attico Fibonacci. I think I loved you from the first moment I saw you. I know I did."

She saw tears glint in his eyes, the depth of emotion in them intense. "I love you, Temple Dubois, and I'm so honored by you being in my life, by you saying yes to becoming my wife. I swear, I will always, always protect you."

Now, as Temple felt terror and hopelessness creeping into her mind, she struggled to hold on to that promise he made. "Attico ... where are you?"

She froze as she heard a door open and a blast of fresh air swept across her hot skin. Someone was there, picking her up, holding a cool glass of water to her lips. She drank gratefully.

"What did you give her?"

Temple tried not to gasp. There were two of them and when the other man, the man who was holding her up, spoke, she felt her heart fail. Of course. Of course it was *him* ...

"Heroin. Little Miss Goody Two Shoes deserves to be brought down a peg. And it keeps her quiet." Brett Forrester. *Of course* ...

The other man whose voice she didn't recognize sighed. "He told us to keep her quiet, not turn her into a junkie."

"What does it matter? She'll be dead soon, anyway."

Temple knew she should feel terror or shock at his words but instead, she just felt resigned. They were going to kill her and she would never know why. And who was the mysterious other man they were talking about? Their boss?

"Exactly. So we don't want her overdosing before we have a chance to put that dagger in her gut, do we? Fuck's sake, Forrester."

"No names," Brett snapped and despite herself, Temple laughed softly.

"I know your voice, Brett, you moron."

She heard the other man laugh in the second before Brett struck her hard enough to make her ears ring. "Don't hurt her."

She felt Brett being pulled to his feet, then someone else sat down beside her. "Go get some food for her." She heard Brett leave the room.

She flinched as the man touched her head. "If I remove this blindfold, you'll see my face. You won't know me, beautiful girl, so don't think it means anything. I'll untie your hands but don't try anything. You'll be dead before you even think about it."

Temple began to tremble as he untied the blindfold and felt the binds on her wrists release. Her shoulders were burning. She blinked in the sudden light. They were in a basement room, somewhere she didn't recognize. It smelled old and damp and she could see dirt and cobwebs everywhere.

The man with her was studying her. She guessed he was in his late forties, which would make sense if he was friends or acquaintances with Brett. Silver shot through his dark hair; he had a Scandinavian lilt to his accent. His brown eyes were watchful, his mouth wide and sensual. Temple found herself staring back at him. "Was she ... the girl, back then ... was she ..."

"No. I didn't know her personally. I was just asked to kill her." He smiled. "Which I did."

Temple felt weak. "Luc?"

"Was simply in the wrong place at the wrong time."

Temple turned and threw up onto the floor. The man, the killer, rubbed her back almost sympathetically. Temple felt both a crushing weight and an overwhelming relief. Weight because she was going to die and she would never see Attico again; relief that her beloved Luc hadn't been a killer. "So why? Why are you going to kill me? Why kill Luc, Olivia ... why try to kill Lucinda?"

"I was hired to torment you, pretty girl, to make you scared, to run into the arms of your billionaire. If it's any consolation ... this isn't about you."

Temple gave a sarcasm smile. "It's not, asshole."

He chuckled. "What a waste it'll be when you die, Miss Dubois. You really are an exquisite woman."

"Fuck you. And it's Mrs. Fibonacci."

He smiled icily. "Well, Mrs. Fibonacci, I assume you require the use of a bathroom?" He nodded to a small door she hadn't noticed before. "In there. And it has no window, so don't even think about trying to escape. There's a toilet, a shower. We'll bring you food and water."

"Until it's time to kill me?"

He smiled. "Until it's time to kill you."

"You still haven't told me why."

He laughed. "Only my employer knows why, Mrs. Fibonacci. I just get the pleasure of carrying out his wishes." His eyes dropped to her breasts, swept over her body. "I'll enjoy it, beautiful girl, but yes. What a waste."

And he was gone.

CHAPTER NINETEEN

Attico leaned his head against the cool glass of the window. Nothing. No news. Temple had just vanished. He had come to her old apartment, one she still rented for some reason, and now he was sitting amongst boxes of her stuff she hadn't yet moved. They hadn't decided where to live when Attico moved to Geneva but even as small as it was, he could see them staying here. It was her place, the place she had chosen for herself to live in, and, even more so now, it seemed vital to him that he honor her choice.

He sighed. "Where are you, baby?"

The police had no leads and even his own team, well-funded and vast, could find nothing. Tony was working all hours to call in favors, reaching out to contacts, but Temple was simply nowhere to be found.

Attico felt useless. He had all the money in the world but nothing would bring her back. Whoever had her ...

They're going to kill her, I know it ... He started as someone banged on the door of the apartment and he got up to let them in. Tony handed him a bag of fast food and a bottle of water. Attico followed him into the kitchen. Tony took off his jacket and sat down. "Atti, eat. Drink. You look a mess."

"Any news? Anything?"

Tony shook his head. "Nothing, brother, I'm sorry. But we're not giving up, I promise you."

Attico shoved his chair back and stood up. "How? How, in this day and age can a woman go missing and ..."

He was aware he was ranting and stopped. "Tony ... do you think she's already dead?"

"No. No, Atti, I don't at all. Temple is stronger than you think."

"Just ... why?"

"The only thing I can think of is that it has to do with Luc. The girl who died—I have someone working on finding out who she was. Yes, her family hushed it up, but we have enough money to bribe whoever we need to. Don't worry."

"Legally?"

Tony half smiled. "Do you care?"

"Not really. Jesus, Tony ... she's just a kid."

"She's a woman, Atti, your wife. I'm telling you, wherever she is, she's trying to figure out a way back to you."

TONY WAS RIGHT. Within an hour of finding out she had access to a bathroom, Temple had gone through every possible mode of escape. Anything she could use as a weapon. A loose tile. A window.

And found nothing.

She had figured out by now that she was deep underground ... but underground where? She used all her senses, even inhaling deeply to see if she recognized any scents. But nothing came to her and now she had slumped back on the small, uncomfortable bunk. *Don't give up hope,* she told herself over and over, but it was hard not to feel despair. She was to be murdered for a reason she didn't know and that was the worse feeling. Luc hadn't killed the girl, so revenge was out, and she realized now that she had been expecting someone to come for her all of her life, to make things right for the girl's family. Maybe that had been another reason why, until Attico, she hadn't been close to anyone, to protect those she loved from danger. She'd failed in that. Luc, Olivia, Lucinda.

And all since she'd been with Attico, which told her something. Attico was the real target, he had to be. The thought of anything happening to him made her want to scream. So she did, screaming until her throat hurt, as long as she could before she sank to the floor, utterly spent.

A few minutes later, Brett Forrester burst through the door. "Shut your damn mouth, bitch." He cuffed her viciously around the face then as she slumped to the floor, he began kicking her, hard, his boot slamming into her stomach again and again.

Temple took the blows again and again, glad as it happened, because behind Brett, the door was open and it told her everything. Outside her tiny prison, she saw the hallway, and the stone walls of her home since she was eight years old.

She was in the catacombs beneath the Academy. They had been rumored, certainly, but no one had ever found where they were. Only, obviously, someone had. Temple knew then what their plan was. She'd be tied to the same lamppost as the girl, killed the same way, a knife buried deep in her belly. As Brett hauled her up and threw her onto the bunk, Temple found her voice again. If she was going to die, what did it matter whether it was then or now?

She screamed at the top of her lungs, hoping someone, some-where would hear her but then Brett delivered the coup de grâce, a vicious blow to her head, and she fell back, stunned.

"Fucking bitch." Brett fumbled in his pocket and pulled out a syringe. He plunged it into her arm and Temple immediately felt the rush of opiates through her system. She went limp, unable to make sense of her thoughts, or reason.

Darkness swirled but not before she heard another voice, a familiar voice. "What the fuck did you do to her?"

"Just gave her a little something to shut her up."

"She looks like hell ... you beat her, asshole."

"She was screaming."

"You dumb fuck."

In her confused state, Temple felt a hand on her face, a gentle hand, almost tender. "It's okay, Tem, it'll all be over soon."

That voice ... so familiar, so kind ... who?

She gave into the darkness which overwhelmed her.

CHAPTER TWENTY

I t was almost midnight when Tony came to find Attico. "Atti, we may have something."

Attico felt his heart leap when he saw the expression on his brother's face. "What is it?"

"It could be nothing, but Brett Forrester was seen going into the Academy. Dean Corke finally revoked his access but someone is getting him in ... and we all know he has history with abusing Temple. It's flimsy, but it's a lead."

As he finished speaking, Attico's phone bleeped. He opened the message and his face drained of blood. "Oh God, no ... Tony ..."

He showed his brother the message. The tarot card that had haunted him since Temple's abduction. The girl bound to the stake, the sword running through her, blood streaming down her dress ... "Tony ..."

He was out of the door before his brother could react.

TEMPLE FELT HERSELF BEING CARRIED. Her head still whirled; they'd given her more drugs, enough to keep her compliant but not enough to knock her out. Not enough to dull the pain. She was being carried by the assassin now, Brett following behind him, his mood significantly cheerier because he knew, and Temple knew, they were taking her to the killing ground. There was tape over her mouth now and her hands were bound behind her back. She wondered how much it would hurt, how long it would take her to die. She felt curiously dispassionate about it.

No one was coming. There was no one to save her.

ATTICO DROVE them at high speed towards the Academy, Tony sitting next to him talking to the police. When he ended the call, he looked at Attico.

"Atti, they're on their way to the Academy. They've notified Dean Corke, and he has his security team out looking for Forrester."

But when they reached the Academy, the whole place was deserted. "What the hell?" Tony stalked the corridor to Dean Corke's office, Attico close behind him, almost frantic now. He felt in his bones—Temple was close, so close.

He almost walked into Tony as his brother skidded to a stop. "Oh Jesus ..."

Dean Corke was slumped over his desk, his eyes sightless and staring, his white hair soaked with blood from a wound on the top of his head. Attico felt his heart stop. "Oh my God." He went to the old man's side and pressed his fingers against his neck. Nothing. "He's dead."

Tony, looking sick to his stomach, let out a shaky breath. "Looking at that wound, he would have died instantly."

Attico shook his head. His eye had been caught by something on the desk, written in blood. "No, he didn't die straightaway. He was trying to tell us something."

"What?"

Attico pointed at the desk and Tony got closer. In blood, one word.

Roof.

. . .

TEMPLE FELT herself being propped against the lamppost and tied to it with long plastic ties. Her feet and hands were bound and her captors wrapped a rope around her under her breasts to keep her upright. Brett seemed to enjoy that in particular, using it an excuse to touch her. His hands dropped quickly when the assassin brought a tire iron down on them. Brett almost screamed in pain, one arm most definitely broken. "What the fuck, man?"

"You don't touch her again," the man told Brett, his voice like ice. "This is not what this is about. You will treat her respect."

He looked at Temple as he fastened her bindings. "I'm sorry about him. I would not have you treated with such disrespect."

Temple, her mouth taped, gave him a withering look, hoping he would understand her scorn. He was about to kill her and he was talking about disrespect?

Her would-be-killer smiled. "You don't believe me?"

Next to him, Brett, still cursing, bent double, holding his broken arm, sneered at them. "Stop sweet talking and stab her for chrissakes. Make it count—you need to hit her artery first time. He only wants one stab wound in her."

The assassin smiled at Temple and then, quick as lightening, lashed out with the knife. Brett stared at him disbelieving as the tip of the knife sliced through his jugular vein. For a second, time stopped, then blood gushed from Brett's neck and he dropped, convulsing on the ground as he bled out. The assassin calmly wiped the blade on Brett's clothes and returned his attention to Temple.

Temple felt a strange calm descend over her. It was time.

ATTICO BEAT Tony to the roof and as he burst through the fire escape door, he came to a halt. This was the place Luc Monfils had jumped from. And now there was no one else here. Not just the roof; according to Tony this place should be crawling with their security teams, the Academy people, the police ... where the hell were they?

He looked for his brother now, saw him standing across the roof, staring down. Tony turned as he approached, his face a mask of horror. "Atti ... look ..."

Attico stared down to where he was pointing. In a pool of light, in the center of the quad, Temple was bound to the lamppost. Attico's heart stopped as the man with her looked up towards Attico, smiled ... and calmly plunged a knife deep into Temple's stomach.

"*No!*" Attico's heart failed as he saw's Temple's head rolled back, agony on her beautiful face, blood beginning to spread across the fabric of her dress. Her killer left the knife embedded in her body, removed the tape from her mouth, kissed her softly, and then calmly walked away into the night. Attico darted back to the fire escape and found it locked. "Fuck, no ..."

Behind him, Tony pulled out his phone and dialed. "Chief Renard, please hurry, the Academy ..." He sounded as panicked as Attico felt as Attico tried everything to open the door, desperate to get to his dying wife. "*Renard, please, please.*"

Attico heard Tony started to sob. "*Renard ... my brother just murdered Temple Dubois ... he killed her and now he's threatening to jump off the roof...*"

Shocked to his core, Attico whirled around as Tony screamed down the phone, "*Atti! No!*"

Tony casually threw the phone over his shoulder, over the side of the Academy, and grinned at his stunned younger sibling. "Surprise," he said, shrugging nonchalantly. "Didn't see that coming, did you?"

And he lunged for his brother.

TEMPLE DRAGGED as much oxygen into her body as she could. *Keep calm, slow your heartbeat down, slow the blood loss.* But already she felt lightheaded, nauseous. She was dying. Keep breathing. She tasted blood in her mouth.

Think of something, anything else but the knife in your belly. The pain was extraordinary, but she forced herself to think of something else. If she was going to die, she wanted the last thought she had to be of Attico. His beautiful green eyes, the way they looked deep into hers, softened with love. "*Ti amo*," he'd said over and over to her. "I love you, I love you."

"I love you, Atti," Temple whispered now. "I'm sorry I left you, my darling love."

She had thought she heard his voice, his shout of horror as she was stabbed, but now she couldn't be sure she hadn't hallucinated it. The drugs they had given her made her unsure of anything except that she was dying.

She moaned slightly from the pain. The way she was bound, she couldn't even move from the standing position. She was on display, bloodied, dying. The cruelty of it overwhelmed her and she let a tear fall down her cheek. *No. Do not give them the satisfaction.* Brett. His body now on the grass in front of her.

Her killer who had kissed her so tenderly then disappeared into the black of night.

Temple drew a shaky breath in. And the man who had arranged it all. She had finally gathered enough of her faculties to identify the familiar voice she had heard in her prison, and it broke her heart.

Tony Fibonacci.

She had been right; it *had* been about Attico the whole time. She would never know why now, but at least she would die knowing who. Tony. He'd killed Luc, Olivia, tried to kill Lucinda, and it had all been for what?

Temple felt a wave of dizziness which didn't relent then as she struggled to stay conscious, she heard his voice again, this time a whisper in her ear, and she knew she was imagining it but she didn't care. "Baby, stay with me, stay with me ... fight, Temple, fight ..."

The darkness took her anyway.

CHAPTER TWENTY-ONE

Attico struggled with his older brother as Tony tried to haul him to the edge of the roof. "What the fuck are you doing?"

"What I should have done a long time ago, Atti." Tony punched Attico, catching him in the temple, and Attico, stunned, slumped to the roof. Tony stood back for a moment, breathing hard. "The story will be this. You were so full of guilt over Luc Monfils that you ended his suffering. You married his sister, with all good intentions, hoping to make up for her life without her family. You fell so deeply in love with her that it was an obsession for you and you planned this. Killing her, then yourself, so you could be together forever."

Attico gaped at his older brother. Tony sounded ... *demented.* "Why? Why all this, Tony? I don't get it. Why?"

Tony smirked. "Oh, poor, poor Atti. So tortured. So beautiful, but so tortured by guilt your whole life. Everything was about you, wasn't it? All the fucking time."

Attico, staggered to his feet, desperate to get down to his wounded wife, opened his hands. "Whatever it is, you can have. My business, my money ... is that it?"

"I don't give a fuck about that."

"Then why?"

Tony smiled. "Because sooner or later, you'd find out who I really am. That girl, Bettina was her name, by the way. I fucked her, and she was stupid enough to get pregnant. The society rallied around me, told me that she was trying to trap me. We meant to kill her. We needed her to die to make the others see that the Winter Blood society meant something more than just a hokey bunch of cards. We're all over the world, Atti. A society of masters. We run everything. Banks, businesses, even countries. Winter Blood is everywhere."

He stepped towards his brother. "But they demand sacrifices, Atti. They solved that problem for me, and now they're asking for payback. They needed proof from me that I was still loyal to them. *You* are my proof."

Attico couldn't quite believe the crap coming from his brother's mouth. "You are insane. Why didn't I see it?"

"Because you're too fucking self-absorbed, that's why! It's always been about poor Attico, beautiful Attico, who never had to try to anything."

Attico lunged at him, tired of hearing Tony's pathetic excuses for the damage he had done, roaring with all the rage, panic, grief he felt. Tony came at him too and they struggled. For a moment, it seemed as if Tony had the upper hand, then, as Attico managed to get his foot planted squarely in Tony's stomach, he hefted his brother up and over the edge of the building. He heard Tony's scream, then his pleading. Attico looked over the edge at Tony, who was clinging by his fingertips to the edge. Below him was a stone ledge and Attico could see Tony's discarded cell phone. The screen was lit up—was the call he'd made to Renard connected? Or was someone calling in?

"Atti ... I'm sorry ... please."

Attico saw Tony's grip slip. He could reach down and grab him, pull him up, leave him to the police, but then an image of the moment Temple had been stabbed flashed through his mind, her lovely face in agony, her blood spilled, and his heart hardened.

"Fuck you."

Tony screamed as his grip slipped and he plummeted to the asphalt below. Attico winced at the wet crunch of his brother's body as it hit the ground, then he was off and running, banging on the locked door of the roof's stairwell, hoping desperately that someone, anyone would hear him. He could hear sirens in the distance and pounded even harder.

It seemed an age before, at last, Chief Renard and his men burst through the door. Attico pushed past them, yelling behind him, "Renard, the quad ... Temple's dying."

He was surprised when Renard accompanied him instead of immediately grabbing and arresting him. As they sped down to the quad, he asked Renard why he wasn't arresting him.

"I'll explain later, Fibonacci."

"They stabbed Temple." Attico felt as if his lungs were going to burst. "They tried to kill her..."

As they ran into the quad, he saw that the police had reached her and were cutting her away from her bindings. They lowered her to the ground as Attico reached them, pushing them out of the way and cradling her in his arms.

"She's alive," said a young policeman, his face pale and sick.

"Don't touch the knife. It might be preventing her from bleeding out," Renard said, crouching beside them. "Get the paramedics in here now."

"They're just coming, boss."

Attico barely heard them. He stared down at her pale, still face. "Baby, please ... fight, Temple, breathe, live ... I love you so much."

He heard a soft moan and his heart leapt as she opened her eyes. "Attico ..." Barely a whisper but her eyes whirled then focused on him. She gave him a sleepy smile. "God, you're beautiful ... I love you ..."

Attico's tears poured down his face. "Promise me you'll live, Temple. Promise me ..."

But her eyes closed and she passed out again and Renard made Attico give her up to the paramedics who arrived. As Temple was being loaded into the ambulance, somebody tapped Attico on the shoulder and he turned.

Denny Fleet nodded to him. "Attico ..."

"What the hell?"

"This is FBI Agent Harry Grant, Attico." Renard was beside him then. "You asked me why I knew Tony was lying. Agent Grant is why."

Attico, almost wild with grief, merely nodded and the FBI agent nodded. "We'll talk more at the hospital, Mr. Fibonacci. For now, go, be with your lovely wife ... and good luck."

ATTICO STARED out of the window of the hospital room, looking out over Geneva. Next to him, in the bed, Temple slept. They'd rushed her into surgery and managed to repair the damage the knife had wrought on her. The blade had missed her abdominal arteries by millimeters and when she'd come out of surgery, the surgeon told Attico that his beloved wife would be okay.

So why didn't he feel joy?

Because this is entirely your fault.

Tony's fucked up reasons for all this ... he would never understand. His father had flown to Geneva to identify Tony's body, had listened to Attico's explanation of what happened, but was utterly devastated by the horror of what happened. Attico could tell his father felt the same guilt that he did. Sebastiano had seemed smaller to him, bent double with grief. Attico had found Sebastiano holding Temple's hand as she lay still asleep from the anesthetic, and somehow knew she was the key to repair the damage in their family.

Denny Fleet—or rather, FBI Agent Grant—had explained who he really was. "The brother of Bettina Lascelles came to us. His parents had hushed up her murder but they had passed on and her brother wanted justice for his sister. No one wanted the case but me. So, reluctantly, I was allowed to pursue the case. My investigations led to your family, Mr. Fibonacci, and at first, I was convinced you were the killer, especially when you married Luc Monfils' sister." He smiled at Attico. "Mr. Fibonacci, at your wedding, which I admit I crashed, I knew I was wrong. No one could fake the love between the two of you. That's when my attention turned to your brother."

He sighed then. "My fatal flaw was that I hesitated, and your lovely wife paid the price, and nearly you too. For that, I am sorry."

Attico shook his head. "It's ... it was Tony. He was insane, and none of us saw it. Everything had to be under his control. It might take us years to figure out why he was ..." He broke off, unable to finish his sentence. "He was all about himself. He knew he wouldn't get away with murder so he tried to cover it up and frame me. I guess blood isn't thicker than water."

"ATTI?"

He turned from the window to see Lucinda, of all people, standing in the doorway. "Lu?"

His shoulders slumped and Lucinda came into the room and hugged him. "Atti, I'm so sorry."

"Lu, what are you doing here?"

She smiled at him, rubbing his arms as if she somehow knew he was cold. "I had to come. Pierre's with me." She looked over at Temple. "How is she?"

"The doc's say she'll be fine physically. The assholes who took her —Tony's men—" Attico closed his eyes, pain searing through him. "They injected her with all kinds of drugs. Heroin, included. She may even need rehab. How fucked up is that? After everything she's been through."

Lucinda went over to Temple and smoothed the hair back from her face. She bent down and kissed the sleeping woman's forehead. "Come back to us, little one. We love you."

Attico felt as if she was saying and doing all the things he should be doing—but no longer had the right to. "How am I ever supposed to look her in the eye again?"

Lucinda looked at him. "This isn't your fault, Atti."

He gave a hollow laugh. "I was never good enough for her. Or you. Or anyone."

"Don't do this, Attico, this isn't helping. When Temple wakes up, she'll need you."

Attico nodded stiffly but said nothing more. He sat down next to Temple's bed and took her hand, feeling how small it was in his hand. He raised it to his lips, kissed it ... and began to sob.

TWO DAYS LATER, Temple opened her eyes. She stared up at the ceiling for a moment before looking around the room. She was staggered to find Lucinda sitting by her bed. The blonde woman looked exhausted, her eyes red-rimmed as she gazed out of the window. "Lu?"

Lucinda looked around and smiled. "Oh darling, you came back to us. How do you feel?"

Temple considered for a moment. "Okay. Sore." She swallowed. "Where's Attico?"

She saw sadness cross Lucinda's face and knew. "He's gone, isn't he?"

Lucinda nodded. "He loves you, but he thinks this is all his fault. I tried to tell him you would want him here ... oh sweetheart ..."

Tears were pouring down Temple's face. "I should never have come back to Geneva. I didn't want to leave him, Lucinda. It was a mistake, and I knew it. I drove him away."

"You did no such thing. This thing was set in motion way before you ever came into the picture. Tony was a jealous asshole—"

"Tony ... God. It was him, the whole time."

"We know, sweetheart."

Temple looked at Lucinda's red-rimmed eyes. "Is he in jail?"

"No, darling. He's dead. He tried to kill Attico, wanted to make it look like Attico had murdered you, and then committed suicide. Trouble was Attico was far too strong for Tony. Tony ... fell from the roof, just like he'd planned for Attico, just like ..."

"Luc. They killed him."

Lucinda nodded. "I know, sweetheart."

"I don't understand why Tony would do all of this."

Lucinda sighed. "They're still trying to unravel it."

"The man who stabbed me ... is he in jail?"

"No, darling, they're still looking for him."

Temple sighed and nodded. Lucinda squeezed her hand. "Are you thirsty? Let me go get you some fresh water."

ALONE, Temple eased herself painfully into a sitting position. Her heart felt heavy, broken. She wanted to see Attico so badly, but she understood the need to run away. Hadn't she done it to him?

"I miss you," she whispered. She saw her bag, packed with her things in the nightstand, and opened it. The large manila envelope was on top. Inside of it were a bunch of papers, signing over owner-ship of the Geneva and New York apartments to her, plus details of a bank account in her name with almost a billion dollars in it. Temple felt numb as she looked at them. "You lied," she whispered to him, but she knew he was just trying to make amends. Another letter told her all her medical bills past, present and future were being taken care of.

But it was the handwritten letter which took all her attention.

MY DARLING, *darling Temple,*

I LOVE YOU. *That's the most important and truthful thing I can say in these circumstances. I love you more than anyone or anything in this world. You are my world.*

But I no longer deserve to be in yours, and I don't know that I ever did. It's my fault that you're lying in this hospital bed and for that, I can never forgive myself.

You are better off without me and so I ask you, my love, to please let me go.

Someday you'll meet someone who can love you the right way, without all this history, without all this hurt. By now you know that I was the one who turned Luc into the police. I misunderstood his role in the death of that poor girl and I will never forgive myself. I wanted to be the one who gave you a real family—instead I was nearly responsible for you losing your life.

It will haunt me forever.

I'm sorry I'm ignoring our prenup, sweetheart, but I have to make sure you're okay. I never meant for us to part, not ever, but now I know it's for the best.

I'm sorry for everything, my darling, but not for loving you. You were the best thing in my life–I just didn't realize I was the worst in yours.

I LOVE YOU, Temple Dubois.
Forever,

ATTICO.

TEMPLE READ the letter through twice then set it down ... and burst into tears.

CHAPTER TWENTY-TWO

S ix months later ...
         Mount Lussari Village, Tarvisio, Italian Alps

ATTICO THANKED the woman behind the counter and stepped out onto the street. This was his morning routine now. Walk into the village from his mountainside cabin, grab an espresso at the small café, bread and a newspaper from the village store. It was the only human contact he had during the day but he felt he might go mad without it.

His handsome face was covered with a thick dark beard now but it didn't stop the admiring looks from the female tourists and locals alike. Still, he kept up a gruff, impenetrable manner to put them off, disappearing to his cabin. He read, chopped wood for the fire, taught himself how to cook ... and thought endlessly about Temple. Obsessively.

Today, though, today, he had decided that he would distract himself from thinking about her. He had deliberately eschewed having an internet connection at the cabin, knowing he would spend hours trying to find out what she was doing now. So now, as he walked back up the mountain to his home, he was trying his hardest to focus on what chores he had to do around the house.

All of his good intentions disappeared when he saw the SUV parked in his driveway and a slightly built figure, standing on his porch, staring at him. She was huddled in a thick coat but her hair, even longer than he remembered, flowed loose down her back. Her large dark eyes were full of wariness, but also love. She was staggeringly beautiful.

Attico lost the power to speak as he walked closer to her. Temple gave a nervous smile. "Hello, Atti."

Attico stopped. Just hearing her voice was like a balm on his psyche. "What are you doing here, Temple?"

"I came for *you*, Atti."

Those five simple words broke him and he looked away from her lovely face. "This isn't ... you shouldn't be here."

Temple pulled a manila envelope from her jacket and walked to him. "These are divorce papers, Atti," she said, her voice shaking. "All I want is one more night. One more night and if, in the morning, you still don't want me, then I'll sign them and you'll never see me again."

"Is that what you want? A divorce?"

She shook her head, her eyes full of tears. "God, *no*. I want you, Atti, but I don't want you to be unhappy. None of it was your fault."

"Luc ..."

"I would have done the same thing if I'd thought I'd caught a killer. You didn't kill Luc, Atti, Tony did." Her voice was hard then, and she stopped, putting her hand to her mouth trying to control her emotions.

Attico waited. God, he wanted to go to her and take her in his arms and never, ever let her go ...

"One more night," Temple said, "one more night. I'll get down on my knees and beg if I have to. I love you, Attico Fibonacci."

With a groan, Attico lost all his self-control and tugged her into his arms, his lips crushing down on hers, feeling her fingers tangle in his hair. They were both breathless when they finally broke apart.

Without saying anything more, he led her into his cabin, kicking the door shut behind him. Temple, her eyes shining with love, shed her coat, and underneath, she wore the dark burgundy dress she had worn on their first date. Attico felt helpless, all those emotions flooding back.

"Oh ... Tem ..." He grinned suddenly. "Aren't you *cold*?"

They both laughed, breaking the tension, and Temple reached down, grabbed the hem of the skirt and pulled it over her head in one movement. She was naked underneath. "Warm me up, Attico ..."

The need to touch her was too much and Attico swept her up into his arms and into the small bedroom. Tearing off his own clothes, he lay down on top of her as she wrapped her legs around him. "Don't wait," she urged, "I want you inside of me."

She reached down and stroked his already hard cock, then guided him inside her sodden cunt. Both of them felt the tension release as they moved together, kissing, touch, caressing. They drove each other to a shattering orgasm, after which they held each other, talking and kissing.

Attico knew, the second he had touched her, that he could never let her go again and he told her that now.

Temple smiled up at him. "I asked for one more night, Attico ... what I neglected to say was I want that night to last approximately eight hundred thousand hours."

Attico laughed. "That's a very specific number."

"I worked it out, using average lifespans and stuff."

Attico laughed aloud. "Such a little geek."

"You know it. Atti ... let's promise. Let's promise to never be apart again. The happiest day of my life was the day I married you. Promise me you'll never let me go again, and this day will beat it."

He took her face in his hands. "Temple Eleanor Dubois Fibonacci, I promise. I promise I will never, ever let you go again. Ever. I love you more than my own life, Tem."

She was crying now and Attico kissed the tears from her sweet face. She smiled up at him. "As I promise you, Attico Fernando

Fibonacci. I love you so much, Atti." She grinned and tugged at his beard. "And by the way, the beard really does it for me."

He laughed. "I was trying something new."

"And here I thought you couldn't get handsomer."

He crossed his eyes and stuck out his tongue. Temple grinned. "Hot."

"By the way, Mrs. Fibonacci, your math is for shit." He trailed his lips along her jaw. Temple wriggled with pleasure.

"How'd you figure? Oh, that's so good, yes ..." Attico had slipped a hand between her legs and was stroking her clit.

He smiled down at her. "The way you worked it out, we'd both live for another ninety years each."

"And we shall, ha ha ha ... oh ... oh ..."

They were too distracted then to keep teasing each other, and they made love long into the night.

CHAPTER TWENTY-THREE

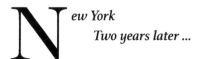*ew York
Two years later ...*

SHE WAS RUNNING, breathing hard, almost frantic now, as her sneak-ered-feet pounded along the corridor of the hospital. Temple ignored all the calls for her to slow down and kept running, desperate, breathless.

Finally, she burst into the room and skidded to a halt. "Oh God ... did I miss it?"

Attico grinned at her. "Afraid so."

Temple groaned and went to Lucinda's side. The blonde woman grinned at her as she lay in the hospital bed, her newborn son in her arms. Pierre, Lucinda's husband, kissed Temple's cheek. "Never mind. We're glad you're here now, little sis."

Temple beamed at him. In the time she and Attico had been back in New York, she had grown ever closer to both Lucinda and Pierre, and the man had become like a brother to her. He reminded her so much of Luc; they even looked similar. She had been glad that he and Lucinda seemed to harbor no resentment for Tony's actions and now, as their son was born, they looked beyond ecstatic.

"Would you like to hold your godson?" Lucinda grinned at Temple, who felt a hot wave of emotion flood through her.

"Godson?"

Lucinda nodded, chuckling and nodding at Attico. "We already asked your hubby. Would you do us the honor of being godmother to our son, Stephen Luc Marmont?"

Temple's eyes filled with tears. "Luc?"

Lucinda nodded and Pierre rubbed Temple's shoulder. "We may never have known him, but we both feel his presence, Tem."

She burst into tears and Attico hugged her, laughing. When she had calmed down, Lucinda handed her godson to her and Temple cradled the baby in her arms. He was so beautiful, so perfect that Temple felt overwhelmed. Attico slid his arm around her waist.

"You look good with a baby in your arms, piccolo."

She smiled up at her husband. "He's gorgeous."

"Can we take that as a yes, Temple?" Lucinda and Pierre were smiling at them.

Temple nodded. "Yes ... yes ..."

LATER, back at their apartment, Temple and Attico sat out on the balcony and watched the sun set over Manhattan. Temple sat on his lap, her head on his shoulder, his arms locked around her. "They named him Luc, Atti."

"I know, baby. It's incredible." He pressed his lips to her hair. "You want one of those?"

Temple chuckled. "One? I want a whole bunch with you. What do you say?"

"I say ... let's get on it." He swept a hand through her hair. "I love you, Temple Fibonacci."

She smiled at him. "Then show me just how much, Attico Fibonacci ..."

And so ... he did.

THE END

ABOUT THE AUTHOR

Mrs. Love writes about smart, sexy women and the hot alpha billionaires who love them. She has found her own happily ever after with her dream husband and adorable 6 and 2 year old kids. Currently, Michelle is hard at work on the next book in the series, and trying to stay off the Internet.
"Thank you for supporting an indie author. Anything you can do, whether it be writing a review, or even simply telling a fellow reader that you enjoyed this. Thanks

🌸 Created with Vellum

Lightning Source UK Ltd.
Milton Keynes UK
UKHW021904100221
378587UK00003B/258